"But there was one secret I never told anyone, one I was absolutely terrified of from the time I was fourteen. A secret I wished would go away; a secret I wanted to shout so everyone would finally know." Carter paused for effect. "I was completely, massively in love with him."

My heart stopped. Fully. The blood rushed to my ears, and I felt like I was having a stroke or living inside some messed-up fever dream where everything was spinning and the world was upside down.

Him. One little word that said so much. Him.

**DREAMSPUN
DESIRES**

Dear Reader,

Love is the dream. It dazzles us, makes us stronger, and brings us to our knees. Dreamspun Desires tell stories of love featuring your favorite heartwarming heroes, captivating plots, and exotic locations. Stories that make your breath catch and your imagination soar.

In the pages of these wonderful love stories, readers can escape to a world where love conquers all, the tenderness of a first kiss sweeps you away, and your heart pounds at the sight of the one you love.

When you put it all together, you find romance in its truest form.

Love always finds a way.

Elizabeth North

Executive Director
Dreamspinner Press

Veronica Cochrane

NEXT TO ME

DREAMSPUN
DESIRES

PUBLISHED BY

DREAMSPINNER
PRESS

Published by
DREAMSPINNER PRESS

5032 Capital Circle SW, Suite 2, PMB# 279,
Tallahassee, FL 32305-7886 USA
www.dreamspinnerpress.com

Next to Me
© 2021 Veronica Cochrane

Cover Art
© 2021 L.C. Chase
http://www.lcchase.com
Cover content is for illustrative purposes only and any person depicted
on the cover is a model.

Paperback ISBN: 978-1-64108-250-1
Digital ISBN: 978-1-64405-892-3
Library of Congress Control Number: 2020947231
Paperback published January 2021
v. 1.0

Printed in the United States of America
∞
This paper meets the requirements of
ANSI/NISO Z39.48-1992 (Permanence of Paper).

VERONICA COCHRANE is a contemporary m/m romance author. She penned her first story at age five, about her childhood best friend and a neighborhood cat. Many years later, she rediscovered her love of writing but is unfortunately no longer a feline enthusiast. Please don't hold that against her.

Veronica is an avid reader and a lifelong romantic. She loves seeing characters fall in love, overcome realistic obstacles, and find their happily ever after. When she's not writing, Veronica enjoys traveling to places with beautiful scenery, and seeing concerts and other live events. Veronica lives in Toronto, Ontario, with her husband.

Twitter: @veronicacwrites

Email: veronicacochrane@outlook.com

By Veronica Cochrane

DREAMSPUN DESIRES
Inevitable Duets
Next to Me
Dance with Me
Rhythm of Us

Published by **DREAMSPINNER PRESS**
www.dreamspinnerpress.com

Acknowledgments

I AM a firm believer, in every aspect of my life, that art is a team effort. The silent voices and cheerleaders behind the scenes are as integral as the creator, and I am incredibly grateful to all those who have made this story what it is.

First and foremost, I would like to thank my husband. Thank you for encouraging me to keep "tip-tip-tapping" on my keyboard and pursuing my crazy idea to start writing again after so many years.

Thank you to the entire team at Dreamspinner Press for your support through this process. Your guidance and professionalism has been such a blessing, and you have made this piece even better than I could have imagined.

Finally, thank you to the reader for choosing to spend your time with characters that I love so much.

Author's Note

CHASE and Carter's story is one that has been at the back of my mind for many years. A narrative of artistic collaboration through friendship and then romance is one that is close to my heart. Their struggle with the realities of dating within the entertainment industry parallels many relationships, including my own love story. I wanted to portray this with as much honesty as possible.

Finding a balance between multiple passions, work, and love isn't always easy. But sometimes, as with Carter and Chase, it just takes a little creativity to find a solution. And when you do, boy is it worth it!

I hope you enjoy the journey.

With love,
Veronica

Chase

Five Years Ago

THE final bell had just rung, signaling the end of class for another day. All the students rushed from the classroom, pushing and shoving each other to get out first, as though the extra minute and a half of weekend would make all the difference. I hung back, slowly putting my books away, delaying this particular weekend as long as possible. I slumped up to my best friend Carter's locker in time to see him cramming the last few items into his bag and closing it for good.

"Hey," I mumbled to him.

"Hey," he said in an equally dejected tone.

"Want to come over to play Xbox?"

"Sure. Gotta kick your ass one last time," he said, though the joke didn't quite triumph over the horribleness. "I can't stay late, though. Gotta finish packing."

I made a sound somewhere in the realm of agreeing with him.

Carter's dad was in the military. They had been stationed here since he was little, but the luck permitting them to stay in one place for so long had run out. They were leaving tomorrow for Massachusetts.

I didn't want him to go. I was fairly certain that he didn't want to move away either. Who wants to transfer with a month and a half left of junior year and have to start fresh for what little remained of high school?

He was one of the few good friends I had. Being painfully shy and openly gay in high school explained that. The growth spurt I had counted on never materialized, so I was also shorter and scrawnier than most of my classmates. Not exactly a winning combination all around, but Carter never seemed bothered by what others thought of me. We had been friends since before elementary school, when he first landed in our town and his family moved into the house next to mine.

We grudgingly made our way to my house, kicking stones along the way to fill the silence that descended between us. We got to my place, took off our shoes, and left our backpacks on the floor in the entryway.

My older brother had left for college the year before, so we had a couple of blissful hours to ourselves until my parents got home from work. I threw a frozen pizza in the oven and pulled out a couple of Cokes for us while we waited for our snack to cook.

"It's gonna be fine, man. We can text every day. Mom says we can come visit in the summer. We're both gonna be in the city in a couple years anyway. Maybe we can even rent a place together or something?"

"Julliard has dorm rooms," I said, being deliberately obtuse and difficult.

How could I tell him that I couldn't live without him, even temporarily? I needed him in my life every day. The way it'd always been.

Carter wasn't just my best friend. I'd been in love with him for as long as I could remember. But he was straight, and I had mostly accepted that. I mean, he had never really dated, but he was so focused on his music he didn't have a lot of spare time. Either way I didn't have any reason to suspect he was anything other than straight. Sometimes I would catch him staring at me when he didn't think I was looking, or he would stand a little closer to me than any of the other guys or hug me a little tighter. But that was only because we had always been in sync. Every so often I could swear there was something there on his side too, though I chalked it up to my imagination playing tricks on me because I wanted it to be true so badly.

Carter was tall and good-looking. He had chestnut-brown hair, and he had somehow missed the teenaged gangliness that wreaked havoc on so many of us. He was outgoing and popular. He had a band, and they actually had paying gigs already, which basically made him a rock star at our school.

I was in the front row for every show he played. Sometimes there were more guys on the stage than in the crowd, but that never stopped him from getting up there and giving his all in front of whoever was sober enough to listen. He was good. And because I played music too, I could tell just how good he was.

"Well, after that," Carter continued. "Or whatever. Maybe we won't live together, but at least we can see each other whenever we want. It's not like I'll never see you."

His reasoning was solid, and you couldn't fault him for trying, but over a year away might as well have been forever as far as I could see it.

Fortunately the oven timer went off before I was forced to respond. I made busywork of pulling the pizza out, grabbing napkins, and doling out slices for us. I slammed the pizza cutter down with a little more force than strictly necessary.

"Chase?" He stepped closer to me and put his hand gently on my shoulder. My back hit the counter. "Let's try to make the most of tonight, okay?" Carter went on. "I just want one more night with my best friend."

The way he was looking at me made me weak in the knees. It was the look he sometimes gave me that let my mind convince me he might feel the same way I did. His pleading eyes stared straight into mine. I had a hard time denying him anything. My brain was slow and foggy, and I couldn't think with him so close to me. I felt myself being pulled toward him, an unconscious movement I had no ability to control. My eyes began to close; I couldn't stop them.

I had never kissed anyone before, and as far as I knew, he hadn't either. This was all gut instinct taking over, without my thinking or overanalyzing. This was my one chance, and if I didn't take it now, I might never get another shot.

I brushed his lips faintly with mine, so lightly it barely even qualified as a kiss. For one perfect second, all was right with the world. And then he tensed and pushed me away aggressively.

"What the fuck, Chase?" he said with uncharacteristic forcefulness.

"I… I…."

I couldn't find the words. I started to break down. Tears formed slowly and began dripping down my heated cheeks before I could stop them. My body started to shake uncontrollably.

"I thought maybe you…." My voice cracked on a sob.

"Were what? Gay? I've always been cool with the gay thing, but I'm not a fucking cocksucker like you."

He walked angrily to the door, stomped into his shoes, and threw his backpack over his shoulder.

"Wait, C, please stop!" I pleaded, my heart breaking into a thousand bits.

He turned back to look at me as he opened the door. He shook his head. And then he was gone.

I fell completely to pieces on the floor of the hallway.

Chase

SUNDAY nights in Ty's living room had been a thing since the first month I'd known him. The people on the periphery were always changing. Partners came and went constantly, as was the way for a group of college kids in their early twenties, but the core group was the same. Sometimes it became a movie night, or we would play poker for money we didn't have. More often than not, it was drinking, and bitching about school and whoever wasn't in the room. It was such a regular event in our lives that it wasn't even a question of making plans anymore; we just kind of all showed up around the same time every week.

The venue had stayed consistent over the years. Ty was one of the lucky ones, or unlucky ones, depending on your perspective, who had parents in the city he could still live with. Ty's parents owned this reasonably-sized duplex in Queens. He lived in a suite in the basement that was freezing in the winter and unbearable in the summer, but saving the cost of renting in Manhattan more than made up for the temperature and the commute.

I'd met Ty a couple of years ago on what was supposed to be a date. Five minutes in, we knew it was never going to be a romantic thing, but it ended up turning into something I needed just as badly. Friends are difficult to find in the city, especially with the insane competition in Julliard, so I was more than happy to have Ty slot me into his group without any sort of hesitation. And it had been that way ever since. I wasn't the most outgoing guy in the world. To have friends who got that and still wanted me around was something I appreciated more than they knew.

This week we had all pitched in for some Chinese food from the little hole-in-the-wall down the road, and we were half watching the *Grammy Awards*, half watching our friend Graham graphically overshare about his hookup with some girl at a bar the night before. I was sitting on the floor with my back against the hideous green-and-yellow floral wingback chair Hannah was in, concentrating on getting the noodles out of the paper take-out container I was holding rather than on G's overdetailed charade.

Chopsticks never seemed to come naturally to me, and fighting with my dinner seemed like as good a distraction as any. I had tried to get my friends to change the channel at least three times, but subtle suggestions clearly weren't working, and pointing it out again would have undoubtedly raised red flags. I was trying hard not to pay attention to the screen, but the universe seemed to get a special kick out of conspiring against me.

"Oh, turn it up!" Cara said, finally cutting Graham off, to everyone's relief. "Ethan Taylor's on!"

Graham slumped back into his seat, muttering to himself, while Ty grabbed the remote and increased the volume on country music's heartthrob introducing the award for the Best New Song. I focused on my noodles, hoping nobody would notice me, trying to use the power of my mind to make what the critics were all predicting not come to be.

"And the award goes to... Inevitable Thorns for 'Next to Me'!"

Of course it was. The band was young, and their star had been rising solidly over the past year or two. They had strong instrumentality and moderately passable lyrics. They also had Carter West as their lead singer. The sexiest man in existence, with the most incredible singing voice I've ever heard. Thorns were bound to go far.

Fortunately for me, everyone in the room seemed to lose interest as soon as Ethan Taylor was no longer in the spotlight, and they immediately began discussing Ethan's upcoming concert tour dates and whether we should scrape together the money to try to get tickets. They largely missed my former best friend bounding down the aisle with his band to collect their prize.

My noodles were churning inside my stomach, making me nauseous. I had a mild stalking/feigned-disinterest relationship with the Thorns in general and the publicly known version of Carter specifically. While I had purposely avoided seeing them live, they seemed to perform at larger and larger venues each time I heard about them. Their recent album generated a huge amount of publicity, and my understanding was that they had been on a national tour for the last several months, playing decent-sized concert halls and small stadiums. Again, feigned disinterest.

I kept half my attention on the TV, which I tried to appear to ignore. Had any of my friends even glanced my way, they would have seen my tense posture and known something was up, but the debate in Ty's living room was getting lively, and Jonathan threw a dumpling at Cara in mock protest about something. Nobody was even paying attention to the show anymore.

On the monitor, Inevitable Thorns had finally made their way onstage after all the handshakes and hugs on the way from their seats. This was their first Grammy, a momentous occasion for any band. I tried to feel happy for them. They collected the award from Ethan Taylor and stood in a semicircle around the microphone. The man I had spent the last five years religiously avoiding, who had at one time meant more to me than anyone else ever could, was in the center, getting ready to speak. The crowd went wild again when Carter raised the trophy above his head, drawing the attention of my friends back to what was happening on the TV.

"Winning this award, for this song especially, means more to me than I can ever say," Carter started, his voice full of emotion.

I knew that look too well. The years might have aged him, built his confidence alongside his talent, and certainly hadn't hurt his looks, but it was the same expression he wore when he got busted for tying Matty Smith's shoelaces together under his desk in the fourth grade and had to sit inside all recess. All the underlying emotion I had always been able to read so easily but that he kept hidden from the world. Whether it was our fourth-grade teacher or the millions of people undoubtedly watching him like we were now, he was clearly feeling something more profound than he was going to let anyone see.

"I grew up in a tiny little town, a nothing town called Stablecreek, Pennsylvania," he continued shakily and then paused to collect himself while a few of the audience members whooped and hollered, not picking up on the seriousness of his sentiment.

Graham and Jonathan both turned to me from their chairs in unison. Uh-oh. Graham opened his big, stupid mouth.

"Hey, isn't that where you're from, Chase? Do you know Carter West? Fucking holding out on us...."

Ty gave me a funny look. He was the only one of the group I had told this story to, though I had never disclosed a name. Ty was smart. I could see he was piecing it together. I shot him a pleading look, begging him not to say anything.

"Shh, I want to hear this," Ty said, frowning at Graham, and everyone slowly focused their attention back on the TV. I gave a silent sigh of relief and mouthed "Thank you" to Ty. I knew I was in for an interrogation later, but having Ty question me on his own would be a thousand times easier than having to explain everything to the full group. Especially when the guy who crushed my heart got everything he had ever dreamed of thousands of miles away and all I could do was watch him anonymously on a television screen.

"I had a best friend when I was young. A friend who lived right next door—next to me," Carter continued from the stage, purposely using the name of the song so everyone knew where this was going. "Our parents were close. Sometimes it was like we were all one family. Through every scraped knee or bad grade or teenage act of rebellion, he and I were together."

A chuckle rose when Carter admitted his childhood infractions to the live audience. On the other side of the country, unbeknownst to him, it was like everything in my world had stopped. All that existed was Carter at the microphone and me staring at him from Ty's living room. My heart was beating quickly, and I'd lost the ability to school my emotions. I put down my damn chopsticks. All I could do was listen to him.

"We knew each other better than anyone. We told each other all our secrets. Where every candy bar was hidden after Halloween. Every dent on the family car that I may have caused." He paused while the audience laughed again.

"But there was one secret I never told anyone, one I was absolutely terrified of from the time I was fourteen. A secret I wished would go away; a secret I wanted to shout so everyone would finally know." Carter paused for effect. "I was completely, massively in love with him."

My heart stopped. Fully. The blood rushed to my ears, and I felt like I was having a stroke or living inside some messed-up fever dream where everything was spinning and the world was upside down.

Him. One little word that said so much. Him.

My thoughts were racing, and they were also completely silent. My body was stuck to the ground and floating ten feet in the air. I was elated. I was terrified. I was completely unable to process this information because it didn't make any sense. *Him?*

Carter was into guys. And there was a him. Could the him have been me? Based on what he'd said—neighbors, secrets—there was no way he was talking about anybody else, but it couldn't have been me either. Could it?

The silence in the theater where he was speaking gave way after a second of processing time to a few lone cheers and "awwws" and grew quickly to the full audience applauding. It's not every day that a rock star winning a Grammy Award comes out of the closet on stage during his acceptance speech. Eventually Carter moved his hands to shush the crowd so he could finish. A few of his bandmates patted him on the back in support.

He stared straight at the camera, straight at me through all the distance, and concluded, "Chase, I know we've lost touch, but this song is for you. I would love to hear from you and to make things right. And to everyone out there struggling with yourselves, or feelings you don't know what to do with, don't wait until you're in your midtwenties and have just won a Grammy to say something. Thank you."

The room around me fell still. Ty reached for the remote and turned off the TV after a moment. They stared at me while I gawked at the blank screen.

Ty seemed to sense my discomfort and silently ushered all of our friends out the door. There were so many questions in everyone's glances, but I couldn't form words or even look away from the television. When we were finally alone, Ty stood and reached to pull me up.

"You need to say something eventually, Chasey," he said gently.

I sighed. "Yes," I said, confirming Ty's unasked question. "He was the one I told you about."

Ty wrapped his arms around me tightly. I was so numb I couldn't even get it together enough to grip him back. He pulled away after a moment.

"But isn't this a good thing? Hell, the man is one of the sexiest musicians out there, and he just confessed to the whole planet that he's gay and he's in love with you!"

"Was," I said. "Was in love with me. At a time when I wanted one person, any person, to understand or get it. He was my best friend, Ty. He could have said something at any point growing up and not made me feel so alone. He could have not basically spat in my face and ignored me for five years. This isn't a new revelation for him."

"He was struggling too, sweetie. And it clearly took him a lot longer than it took you to come to terms with it." He rested his hand on my arm.

"I don't know how to deal with this," I replied softly.

"Sleep on it. Process. Take a couple of days. You're not exactly anonymous with him broadcasting it on TV like that, but decide for yourself if you want to contact him. We've all got your back either way. No judgment." He gave my arm a squeeze.

"Yeah. I'll think about it."

We said our goodbyes. I promised to let him know if I needed anything and left quietly, still completely shaken.

Carter

I OBSESSED over social media for days, waiting for a message from him. Every time a new notification dinged, my stomach dropped and my heart started pounding through my chest. It was always the media, digging for information, or worse, someone claiming to be Chase to try to get a response from me. The latter usually turned out to be bigoted trolls saying horrible words. Or almost as often, someone trying to get in my pants or sending a meant-to-be-enticing-but-actually-disgusting dick pic.

I tried not to be overly cocky about my band's success. For all I knew, Chase hadn't even seen the *Grammys* or heard my speech. So what if we used to watch the *Grammys* together every year religiously when we were growing up? People change. At the time it had felt like the odds of his watching the awards were good, but now I was second-guessing how realistic that was.

Even if he hadn't seen the broadcast itself, the media had been having a field day—first with me coming out, and then with what they saw as me pouring my heart out in a hopelessly romantic gesture. Everyone wanted a piece of me. There was a bidding war to get the first official coming-out interview with me. Fortunately, my amazing publicist was dealing with that one and keeping me out of it. I stayed quiet. Or as quiet as the lead singer in a rock band on their first major tour can.

Cities blended together. Detroit, Cleveland, Toronto. I played my shows without addressing the rainbow elephant in the room, even though it felt like said elephant was sitting on my chest and growing bigger each day.

The more time went by, the more I lost hope he would reach out. The more the pessimistic side of my brain was convinced he had seen my speech and just wasn't interested. For all I knew, he was already married, with a boring accountant husband, a white picket fence, and some disgustingly loyal golden retriever. Maybe they were sipping chardonnay in their oversized porch swing, watching the sun going down and making fun of the pathetic closeted rock star for dwelling on a teenage crush instead of having a love life of his own. I wanted him to be happy. He deserved to be happy. A lot of time had gone by. I didn't even know if he was still in Pennsylvania or what he did for a living.

Even if by some miracle he was single, he simply may have not wanted to talk to me. I have never regretted anything in my life the way I regretted what I did to him. On the spinning wheel of horrible moments in my life, that had the permanent spot of being the worst. Number one with a bullet. It was something I wished I could take back from the moment I said it. But I was young and scared and stupid. I ruined the best thing in my life, and maybe now that I had finally owned up to it, I could move on and let some of the guilt go.

This all-consuming situation needed a resolution. I needed to move on with my life. Focus on my music, finish the tour, write the music for our new album. Maybe even get laid. Something.

After a week, I was fairly convinced I regretted what I'd done. Not the coming-out bit. That was a long time coming. But the part about professing my love on national television for someone who was basically now a stranger? That was a little embarrassing. I was mortified enough by the media frenzy I had caused, so I couldn't say I blamed Chase for keeping quiet. Life in the public was not easy. Despite the success of our first album and tour, I had stayed relatively under the radar until this. But for most people, the lifestyle that came along with being with me would be an automatic deal breaker. Especially now.

We were on the road, wrapping up the last month of East Coast dates. Somewhere between Cleveland and Pittsburgh, I think. It was late, and most of the guys were asleep in their bunks after another high-energy gig. I was staring aimlessly out the window, watching the streetlamps and headlights pass by, every mile taking us closer to our final destination. It had been exhausting and exhilarating. A once-in-a-lifetime experience. Tickets were selling faster since our big win, and the fans seemed to love us more and more in each city we played.

The band were all getting under each other's skin a little now; things that would have slid by back in Oregon were now enough to pick fights over. We needed some time back home, some space to ourselves to recharge, but ultimately we were brothers and knew the road would call us back before too long.

I was half asleep from the gentle sway of the bus, my head against the window and my phone loose in my hand. Any small bump would have caused it to fall, but the quiet ding of an incoming message jerked me awake.

Chase

I MUST have started and deleted messages a hundred times over the week since the awards show. I had been inconspicuously following Carter on social media for years, but it was starting to concern even me how much time I was spending looking at his pages now. I didn't know what to do. How to start. I had been over it and over it: What I wanted to say after so long. What I wanted to happen. How much I was willing to have my heart broken by this man. Again.

Then there were the incoming messages. People I hadn't spoken to for years sending me the link to that damn speech. Acquaintances posing as friends, trying to use whatever angle they thought would work to get close to Carter. God, if this was how it was for me, I couldn't imagine how bad it was for him. Not that it wasn't his fault. He at least had a choice in the matter.

I finally gave up and slammed the lid of my laptop down. I texted Ty, and we agreed to meet at a bar near campus. I needed to talk to someone, and I could count on him not to make a bigger deal out of this than it was.

About an hour later, I looked up over the rim of my beer and saw Ty coming through the door. I wasn't much of a drinker, but I might have one or two socially, and tonight I felt it could only help me to relax.

"Hey." He hugged me in greeting before quickly ordering himself a microbrew from the bartender.

We talked for a minute or two while he waited for his drink, taking a deep pull when it was set in front of him.

"So, what's up?" Ty finally asked.

"I don't know. The whole thing is just so insane, I don't know what to do...." I trailed off, assuming Ty would understand what I was talking about without my actually having to say the words.

Ty made encouraging sounds to keep me going but not interrupt my broken train of thought.

"He was *everything* to me for so long. And to hear him say he felt the same way? How could he have done that? How could he have said those horrible things to me after we kissed if he felt the same? He didn't talk to me for so long. He broke my heart, Ty. And now for him to say all that in front of the world? As part of a sound bite to help promote a song?" I threw up my hands in exasperation.

"It sounds like you still feel something for him, babe. You wouldn't be this worked up if you felt nothing," he said.

"That's the stupid part. I *was* over him. It took me forever to get there, and now it's like I'm right back to the beginning. The day after he left."

"What did you like about him in the first place? When you were kids?" Ty asked, changing the course of the conversation.

I thought for a half second before telling Ty a couple stories about Carter and me when we were young. How caring he was. How protective he was of me when I came out. Some of the stupid pranks he pulled. The music we fought over. Twenty minutes had passed by the time I was done, and I was smiling to myself and laughing at the memories while Ty just sat there, sipping his beer. I finally stopped, noticing the smirk on his face.

"What?" I said, fairly certain I knew what was coming.

"And the bad things about him? Was it that one moment, or anything else he did?" Ty asked.

"Just that. But that one moment changed everything. It broke *everything*. He had five years to reach out and apologize. I understand better than anyone how scary coming to terms with being gay is, but to let *five years* go by?"

"I think you need to talk to him, Chasey," Ty said gently. "You don't have to forgive him right away, or see him again if you don't want to. This will be closure for you. Hear him out, and then you can move on. You're in control here."

I exhaled deeply, knowing Ty was right. If I didn't reach out, I would wonder what would have happened. Nothing more than a conversation had to come from it. I wasn't promising him anything; I was listening to his reasoning about what had happened as a way to reconcile it in my head.

"You're right." I hunched my shoulders. "I guess I need to hear what he has to say."

Ty hugged me, rubbing his fingers along my back soothingly. "And we're all here for you, whatever happens. No matter what."

I got back home with a new determination, having already made the decision to go through with this. I dropped my keys in the bowl by the door and walked into the kitchen to make myself a mug of tea I didn't need this late at night, once again stalling for time. I grabbed my laptop and sat cross-legged on my bed, the mug warming my hands. I opened a new message box on his page, thought about it for a second, and started typing.

Carter

I GLANCED down at the illuminated screen, my eyelids half closed against the brightness. Doing a double take, I was suddenly far more awake than I should have been at this hour. I unlocked my phone and, with hands shaking from too much adrenaline, pulled up the full private message.

> *Hey C. I know it's been a long time, but I saw your speech the other night. Congratulations, C. I'm so proud of you for how hard you've worked and how far you've come with your music. I hope you're doing well besides that. Message me back if you want to talk. Chase*

I read the short message three times in rapid succession. It was annoyingly brief, without really addressing the content of my speech or my massive public confessions, but I was sure it was him from the nickname only he ever called me.

I brought up his profile, and while it was clearly not the profile of a public figure who relied on social media for exposure, there were a decent number of posts and pictures. One from last week: bundled up with the snow falling around him, a scarf around his neck, and his mittened hand around a paper coffee cup, smiling at whoever took the photo. Another one from a month ago: sitting at a piano with his back facing the camera, the beautiful house of a soft-seat theater in the background. A third from last summer: on a sandy beach lying on a brightly colored towel, flanked by two other attractive men. My breath caught at that photo, how much of him was exposed in the tiny swimsuit he wore. He had the same creamy, unblemished skin as always, but there was muscle definition now that hadn't been there in high school. The guys he was with were certainly good-looking but didn't hold a candle to the man in the middle. Chase didn't look to be showing a preference for one guy over the other, so I let out a silent plea that they were both just his friends.

As I looked back further and further through his account, the seasons changed, but his brightness never dimmed. I dreamed about what his life was like through the small clues I found. There didn't seem to be a boyfriend, or at least any one guy he took photos with regularly. He was an undergrad in composition studies at Julliard. I was so happy for him about that. Despite being a professional musician, college had never been in the cards for me, but I had nothing but respect for him choosing that as his path. I remember the day he got accepted into Julliard's summer program when we were in high school. It was such an accomplishment, and he always said that would open doors for studying at the prestigious conservatory that had been his aspiration for so long.

When we were young, we had planned on living in New York City together when we grew up. My primary residence currently was a loft in Chelsea, so I found it interesting that dream had come true for us both separately. Chase had always been determined on what he set his mind to, so I can't say I was entirely surprised he was going after what he wanted. Julliard. Manhattan.

The band was rolling into Buffalo shortly, with two performances at Radio City Music Hall coming up soon. He was only a few days and a handful of cities from where we were now. I went back to the original message thread, surprised my luck was so good.

> *Hey! I can't believe you actually messaged me :). I was wondering if we could get together and talk? I really need to explain myself to you and apologize in person. Can we do that? I'm in New York next week for a couple of shows, please say you'll come?*

I fought to keep my words casual, though I was feeling anything but. I didn't want to scare him off before I could see him face-to-face. I wanted him to have an idea of what I wanted to talk about, but I needed to save the actual apology for when we met in person.

He responded quickly, thankfully, and we arranged for him to meet me before the show on Wednesday. Plans made, I finally relaxed and fell asleep with a lightness that I had been missing for years.

Chase

MY NERVES were shot for the rest of the week. I was anxious and jumpy, unable to focus on anything except seeing Carter on Wednesday. The logical side of my brain knew that I was in the driver's seat. He was the one who had reached out—in front of millions, no less. We were connected by our past, but I could walk away at any time without any major ramifications to my life as it was now. He had left once; I could handle it again. I thought.

My mind was in overdrive, anticipating what he would say, what I could say. The smallest things set me off. I was useless at school and at work. Fortunately there weren't any exams or papers due that week, so at least my GPA was safe from taking a Carter West nosedive.

By Wednesday afternoon when I got home from class, I was ready to get the whole thing over with and move on with my life. I thought about bringing Ty along for moral support, but I hadn't told him I was meeting Carter, and it seemed like the kind of thing I had to do solo.

I showered, made my hair look as good as it was going to, and stood in front of my closet for half an hour trying to figure out what to wear, finally settling on a cream-colored cable-knit sweater that set off the green in my eyes, and my favorite pair of midwash jeans that made my ass look decent but were worn enough to be comfortable. I grabbed my jacket and a scarf, threw on some practical but stylish boots, and headed out the door before I thought too hard and called the whole thing off.

I arrived at Radio City, bypassing the massive line of fans already stretching down the block, and went around the back to the stage-door entrance Carter had directed me to. It was easy enough to find, with two massive trucks featuring the band name and logo in the loading bay next to a locked door with a passcode key. A couple of girls, all done up, were off to the side, probably hoping to get a peek at one of the guys in the band, but apart from that it was deserted. The girls stared at me suspiciously, wondering if I was someone they should recognize or if I might be able to help them get inside. I ignored them and knocked on the door, willing myself not to be an embarrassing sweaty mess when I finally saw Carter.

A massive guy in a well-fitting suit, whom I immediately started referring to as "Barracuda" in my head, opened the door a crack and grunted at me.

"Hi! Cold out tonight, isn't it? The band, well not so much the band, but um, this guy I know, Carter West, told me to come here? I swear I'm not a creepy stalker or anything. I really know him. Well, I used to, I guess. Haven't seen him for a number of years, but he wanted to see me. He told me to be here around seven, but I guess I'm a little early. I can come back later if you want. I mean, not too much later because, um, it's almost seven, and I don't know if he has to, like, get ready or anything?"

Oh God. *Smooth, Chase.* Barracuda stared at me during my idiotic ramblings, like I'm sure he did for every other groupie stalker swearing up and down he knew the band.

"I really know him!" I blurted out to fill the awkward silence, answering my own internal dialogue and inevitably making myself seem like more of a pathetic loser.

"Name?" the guy rumbled monosyllabically.

"Chase? Collins?"

I was so bad at this I couldn't even commit to my name being my name. He checked the clipboard I then saw he was holding in his Goliath-sized palm. He grumbled, opening the door wide enough for me to pass through, and made the slightest nod to affirm that I was, in fact, on the list. I thanked him, and he motioned for me to follow him down the painted cinder-block hallway. We walked through the loading dock—past a couple of other men in the same style of suit, a handful of technicians clad all in black, and a myriad of lighting and sound gear I wouldn't even try to identify—until we started passing dressing-room doors.

The numbers on the doors moved in reverse order, signs with names and the band's logo taped to each one. Two rooms for the opener, then a private room for each member of the band. I recognized their names from unofficially following them online: Beau Davis, Asher Wright, and Dean Phillips. My personal security barracuda led me to Dressing Room 1. The sign proclaimed it belonged to Carter West. My heart was in my stomach, and I felt light-headed. It was a miracle I hadn't sweated through my jacket at that point.

Barracuda rapped firmly on the door. We waited. We waited. It felt like a fucking eternity, but we waited. I was absolutely going to simultaneously vomit on myself and pass out while the waiting continued. Finally the door swung open, and there he was.

I had only a second to look at him before he processed who was standing in front of him, during which time I cataloged the changes between the boy I knew and the man he had become. His jaw was a little sharper now, covered with just the right amount of stubble. His cheekbones were high and beautiful, begging for my thumbs to run over them. His eyes were the same milk-chocolate-colored pools I could get lost in for hours if he would let me. The familiar long eyelashes that both our moms had always been envious of. He had grown a fraction taller. He was always bigger than me growing up, but he was the perfect height now. Tall, but I could still reach his full rose-pink lips if I stood on my toes. Not that there was any chance of that happening anytime soon, I scolded myself. His hair was longer, dark chestnut-brown waves which fell almost to his shoulders, skimming the collar of his worn black leather bomber jacket. Damn. Even after five years without him and his shattering my heart, this man pushed all my buttons without doing anything more than existing.

A grin broke across his face as he recognized me. And just like that, I was sixteen again. Hopelessly and helplessly in love with my best friend. My straight best friend who wasn't so straight anymore, and apparently wasn't back then either.

He tentatively took a step forward, arms open but unsure, hesitation in his eyes but reassurance in his smile. He wrapped his arms around me, and I was enveloped in the smell of his leather jacket and his pine aftershave. Our bodies fit each other naturally, the top of my head effortlessly finding a perfect spot cradled under his chin. I snaked my arms around his back, and we stood there holding each other, letting all the distance and hurt of the past five years go for a moment to just be with each other. I hugged him. I hugged him and breathed him in. I was overwhelmed with emotions; mostly I was happy, but I also remembered at the back of my mind the last time I touched him and how heartbreaking his rejection had been. I refused to get teary, and when I was on the verge of losing that battle, Barracuda broke the tension by clearing his throat.

Carter released his hold on me, stepped back, and thanked Barracuda, giving him his leave. Carter pushed his dressing-room door open, held it for me, and let me lead the way inside.

While I had been in enough dressing rooms and theaters in my life to know the basic provisions, his room was cushier than most of the spaces I had seen. A maroon-colored sofa took up the center of the room, with matching chairs and a glass coffee table rounding out the setup. A TV screen hung on the wall opposite the couch, next to the door, with a live feed to the stage where the opening act would be starting their set shortly. Signed photos lined the walls—past bands and celebrities who had performed here. A small kitchenette at the back wall held some fruit, snacks, water bottles, and the makings for coffee.

The door clicked shut, and I turned to face Carter. I finally relaxed the muscles in my back I didn't know I'd been tensing.

"Hey," he said simply, his face beaming so brightly I forgot anything else existed.

"Hi," I replied, mirroring his smile and hoping I didn't look as stupid as I felt. "It's, uh, it's really good to see you, C."

"Yeah?" he asked, and for the first time I was aware he might be as nervous as I was. "I wasn't sure if you would want to. I wouldn't blame you if you didn't. I didn't think I would ever hear from you again."

"It's been a long time, C. We're not the same people we were when we were sixteen. I don't want to lie. What you did hurt, a lot, and for a long time, but I don't hold it against you now either."

"Can we sit down and talk? I have some things I want to explain; not to excuse what I did, but to maybe help you understand?"

I nodded. He offered me some water, which I took more for something to do with my hands than anything else, and we settled at opposite ends of the sofa.

Carter

"LOOK...," I started nervously, inhaling slowly to collect my thoughts.

I didn't want to fuck this up. I wanted to help him understand and then let him decide what to do with the information. Obviously I had a stake in which way he decided to take what I had to say, but more than anything I just wanted him to finally know the truth.

"I've wanted to reach out for a long time. Years. I didn't know how to start or what to say. That day in your kitchen before I left? What I said? How I acted? I've never regretted anything in my life more than that moment. I'd never told anyone I was gay. Hell, I'd never even said the words out loud. I knew deep down, but I had a hard time acknowledging it."

I paused.

"You were always so comfortable with your sexuality. You had such courage, Chase. You knew who you were from day one, and fuck anyone who had a problem with that. I know how hard it was for you to be out, and I felt like such a coward for not saying anything about myself to take some of the heat off you. It took me a long time to accept myself. It honestly hasn't been until the last year or so that I've been completely okay with it. I told my parents a couple months back. They were surprised, I think, but they were more understanding than I thought they might be. I want to stop hiding. To be at peace with myself. To be a role model. The band is doing so well, and I don't want to lie to little kids out there who might be looking up to me. Hell, I don't want to lie to myself anymore."

"I'm not so brave," Chase said quietly. "It was never easy for me either. There was never an option. It was just what it was."

"I know." I put my hand on his knee in reassurance. "And that's what I always admired so much about you. That being gay was nothing you were ashamed of or wanted to change. It simply was."

"And the other part? You said you were… had feelings? For me?" Chase looked up through his eyelashes shyly, and it was absolutely impossible to see how anyone wouldn't be in lo—have feelings—for him.

"Of course I did," I admitted. "You were sweet and sincere. Adventurous. Funny. Kind. We were best friends. You could talk about music with me in a way that nobody else could. You were everything to me. I had feelings for you for so fucking long. I was just scared, you know?"

Chase nodded, his beautiful cheeks flushed.

"I was wrong to push you away and to call you such a horrible word. I knew it at the time. Everything inside me was screaming at me not to stop kissing you. I had wanted to kiss you forever. I was stupid and scared, and I hated myself for a long time after."

After another pause, I finally gathered up the courage that generally evaded me. "I know we don't know each other anymore, but I want to get to know you again. To make things right. I am so, so sorry, Chase," I said with sincerity, laying everything on the table.

"I want to get to know you again too, C," he said tentatively.

It would take time to fully earn back his trust. I knew that. But I would take whatever he was willing to give to have him back in my life.

"Friends?" I asked.

He nodded. "Friends."

I broke into an embarrassingly big smile, which made him smile back at me. We stared at each other, each of us refusing to drop the other's gaze, until he finally went cross-eyed and stuck out his tongue to get me to break. Our smiles turned into grins, which turned into giggles and then into full-out laughter, the tension from the moment and all the bullshit from the past five years taking a first step toward healing.

After laughing reached the point where it hurt too much to keep going, I leaned in and lowered my voice. "Okay, so I gotta know. Did you ever, you know, think of me... that way? Or was it an in-the-moment thing? Kissing me?"

He rolled his eyes. "Of course I did. But I thought you were straight, and I had... maybe not accepted that but at least respected you enough not to say anything."

"Kinda messed up, isn't it?" I chuckled. "We both wanted the same thing but couldn't do anything about it."

"Yeah." A smirk slowly drew across his face. "God, sixteen-year-old me would be combusting right about now if he knew Carter West was going to admit he had a crush on me. At the *Grammy Awards*, of all places."

It was my turn to roll my eyes.

"Certainly would have made high school more bearable if we had been fooling around," I joked, finally feeling a little lighter and like he was someone I knew again.

He laughed nervously and then replied.

"Is it bad that I'm kinda happy we didn't? I mean, it would have been awesome at the time, but we were a couple of horny and stupid kids. We would have fucked it up, ruined what we had."

"Ooh, so the truth comes out after all these years. You thought I was stupid," I teased.

God, this felt so good. Relaxing and laughing with him again. Even after such a short time, all my feelings for him came rushing back—if they had ever gone away at all. It was always so easy with him. I tried to keep my emotions in check for the moment. Whether something more was on the table was for future us to worry about. It felt so good to have him back in my life again, in any way I could have him. I wanted to focus on that.

"Well, I mean, I wasn't the one who broke my arm falling out of Mr. Harlow's apple tree trying to impress everyone at Timothy Macalbee's Halloween party." He winked.

"The branch broke. Could have happened to anyone," I said, pretending to be offended.

But he continued to bait me. "Annnnd I wasn't the one who only passed sophomore English because I volunteered to play Desdemona for extra credit in the school play when Tina Carlo got stage fright an hour before curtain."

"I was doing Mrs. Burns a favor!"

"You should really tell the rest of your band that story. Make sure they know how multitalented you are. Maybe even do a Broadway play if the rock music doesn't work out," he mused. "There are a lot of stories I could sell to the press now. I do have a bunch of student loans to pay off eventually." He grinned at me.

"Oh, screw you. I've got shit on you too!" I said, lobbing the banter back at him.

The program-sound speaker suddenly coming to life cut off our laughter. "And that's intermission, Thorns. This is your fifteen. Fifteen minutes, guys."

I hadn't realized how long we'd been talking, or that I'd missed the opener's entire set. I normally watched it from the wings, but this perfect guy in front of me made me forget the outside world existed.

"You gotta go?" he asked.

"Yeah, gotta head out there in a second. But can you stay to see the show? It would mean a lot to me if you listened to us play." What the hell, might as well go for it. I still had no idea what his personal situation was, or anything about his life; all I knew was getting him to stay to see the concert and maybe have dinner with me afterward was a good first step.

"Yeah." He smiled at me. "I'll stay."

"Perfect." I couldn't hold back the goofy grin blooming again. What was it with this guy? I never stopped smiling around him.

He grabbed his coat, and I snatched a water on the way out. I headed in the general direction of the stage and found Cory, our manager, in the Green Room on the way. I let him know Chase was going to watch the show and asked Cory to find Chase a seat and for someone to bring him back to my dressing room after we were done. We said goodbye, far quicker than I would have liked, but I made sure to squeeze his shoulder on the way out the door. It wasn't exactly the amount of physical contact I wanted, but God, it felt so good to touch him.

He winked at me before allowing himself to be led in the opposite direction from where I was headed. "Break a leg, rock star."

Chase

I FOLLOWED Carter's manager to the front-of-house area. He was walking quickly, and I was straining to keep up. Things were… surprisingly easy between Carter and me. It wasn't awkward after the first few minutes, and by the end it felt like we were almost back to the way things had been before that last night.

And yet something was there that hadn't been before too. I had always been attracted to him, from the time before I even had a name for it. Now it was… mutual? Or I'm pretty sure it was at least. So much time had gone by. We needed to get to know each other again before we thought about going down that road.

There was also the not insignificant obstacle of him being an internationally known musician. Did I want a life where privacy wasn't always guaranteed? Not to mention the touring. Despite living in New York and planning a career that had a certain amount of profile to it, I was essentially a homebody.

Though I'd never had a real relationship that had lasted more than a few months, I knew casual wasn't my thing. I wanted to come home to my guy at the end of the day. Hide under a blanket in thunderstorms with him. Cook a turkey and laugh about the ridiculous size of it for two people at Thanksgiving. A partner who was gone for months at a time? Being hit on by countless attractive men (and women) who thought he owed them something because they liked his music? I didn't know if I could, or would want to, handle that.

We reached a half-empty row of seats, amazing seats, basically as close to the stage as one could get. Cory (Cody? Colby?) gestured for me to sit and said someone would meet me here after the show. I sat down, put my jacket on the back of my chair, and spent about twenty seconds getting comfortable before the house music abruptly cut out and the lights went down.

The screams were deafening. The energy from the audience made it real. I had purposely not seen an Inevitable Thorns concert. I wasn't sure if I would be able to watch Carter in such an anonymous way without giving him the option of seeing me back. I didn't know if I would be able to handle seeing him sing like a god and move like sex on a stage in front of thousands of faceless fans, knowing he could never be mine.

Carter had always had charisma, was always able to charm his way into an extra cookie when we were kids or, as I had reminded him, talk the drama teacher into letting him play some ridiculous drag version of a Shakespearian damsel to pass a class in high school. A true extroverted introvert, he was the center of attention on the outside, but someone who kept so much of himself internalized.

The collective screaming got louder as the Thorns, minus Carter, made their way to their instruments on the still-dark stage. And then, when they were settled, rising from a trapdoor in the center of the stage floor on some sort of fancy elevator system, there he was. I would have rolled my eyes at the overly dramatic entrance if they hadn't been completely bugged out of my head over how unbelievably sexy he looked. He was facing away from the audience, guitar thrown over his leather-jacket-clad back, wearing a pair of black jeans that I somehow hadn't noticed the tightness of when we were backstage together. *He should just do the entire concert like this*, I thought. His ass in those jeans was well worth the price of admission on its own. Clearly the rest of the audience agreed with me; if I thought the noise was deafening before, it was verging on unbearable now.

Once his platform was level with the rest of the stage, the lights started flashing in a crazy pattern and the drummer counted in the first song. The lights all snapped out, with a single spot focused on Carter as he turned around and started singing the opening notes of the first song into the microphone in front of him.

The thousands of people in the hall became nothing but background noise. We locked eyes, and he was singing only to me. It was a sultry, bordering on dirty, song about relentlessly wanting someone from across the dance floor. I figured he probably always started with this song, but it seemed a little poignant right now with his gaze never leaving mine. His hands caressed the mic stand, his hips keeping time with the beat in a way that left nothing, and everything, to the imagination. He belonged up there. The crowd loved him, and I had no doubt in my mind that this was exactly where he needed to be.

The first verse blended effortlessly into the chorus, the band picking up speed and Carter's voice sailing over the vocal runs. Oh Christ, this was the worst kind of foreplay. My cock perked up in my jeans from his dirty words and his gravelly voice alone. His tight jeans stretched over the significant bulge in the front of his pants. The way he was circling and thrusting his hips subtly with the beat of the song was mesmerizing. Eventually the climax of the song crashed down, the cymbals ringing out over the applause.

I was stunned by how the boy I'd known had transformed into this pure magnetic force on the stage, sharing his gift with the world. Even when we were talking earlier, he was down-to-earth and completely ordinary. If I hadn't known him, had passed him on the street, I never would have predicted he would come alive like this in front of the lights. But I did know him. I knew about the thousands of hours he spent practicing when we were younger. I knew about the hundreds of calls he made to get a handful of gigs at seedy clubs. I knew about the blood, sweat, and tears he had poured willingly into making this happen for himself. Out of all the millions of people wanting to make music for a living, to be the showman at the front of the band, he was talented enough and driven enough to make it happen for himself. I had never been so proud.

Carter

THE show went on in a fairly typical way. Nothing but that one pair of emerald eyes staring at me intently, making it different from any other of the dozens of shows we had played over the past few months. But those eyes were distracting as hell. I stumbled over my words a few times in the first song, forgetting momentarily that it was my job to sing in front of all these paying fans. Fortunately my boys covered for me, and probably nobody on the other side of the stage noticed. Dean, our bass player, shot me a look after the third slip, wordlessly asking what the hell was wrong with me tonight. I tried to focus more after that, reluctantly peeling my sight line off the angel near the front row to focus on the rest of the onlookers.

I stopped about three or four songs in to drink some water, addressing the crowd while I stalled to sip the tepid liquid.

"How's everyone doing tonight?" I spoke into the center microphone.

A cacophony of screams and variations of "good!" echoed back to me. I liked to have a rapport with the audience. Telling some off-the-cuff stories and interacting with the band made it feel like a more personal experience than phoning in the exact same show every night. That was one of the reasons I'd decided on the spur of the moment to open with "Dance Floor" tonight, instead of the song we usually started with. Well, that and I was feeling more than a little inspired by someone I was in a similar situation with.

After a little more stage babble, we launched into the rest of the set, blowing through song after song. Honestly, it was one of the few nights I just wanted it to be over. I so rarely had plans after the show, and more often than not, it was getting on a bus and hightailing it to the next venue while trying to rest my voice as much as possible. The glamorous life of a rock star.

We finally hit what would be the last song of the night. I wanted to introduce this one in a special way while respecting Chase's privacy and not giving away to a couple thousand people that he was actually in the house tonight. I took another swig from my water bottle and started to speak.

"So, this is the last number in the show."

A collective "awww" rose from in front of me.

"I'm sorry! I wish we could stay all night too! We've loved being here with you, New York, and I'm sure we'll be back again soon. This last song's a personal one to me, and we recently won a really big award for it."

Cheers erupted when the audience figured out which song we were going to close with. I unclipped the mic from the stand and walked over to the piano. I shot Beau, our keys player, an apologetic look for impulsively kicking him off his instrument.

While I had always gravitated more to the guitar and considered it to be my primary instrument, I had written this song on the piano, and it always seemed to sit there nicer than anywhere else.

"It's about longing and fear and hope, and ultimately about accepting yourself. It's something I've struggled with for most of my life, but recently, since I've been open about it, I've realized there is far more love in this world than hate. The support I've received from people from every corner of the country has been far greater than the ugly words of the few bigoted trolls who hate me simply because I exist. And yeah, it's taken me a long time to get here, but things are pretty good right now." I looked helplessly at the boy in the front row who had unknowingly inspired my words. "This song is called 'Next to Me,' and like always, this one's for Chase."

I started to play, the first verse only my voice and the keys rising up to soar together, with the band not joining in until the chorus. I hadn't thought through the positioning on the stage when I decided to play this one on piano tonight, but being seated at the piano forced me to sit with my back almost directly to Chase. While I cursed myself for not realizing this, I probably wouldn't have gotten through the song without my voice breaking if I'd been able to sing it directly to him.

Chase

I SAT stiff as a board when Carter started to play "Next to Me," not wanting to miss a note. By the end of the first verse, I was barely holding myself together, only maintaining my composure so as not to draw any attention. I had purposely not listened to the song since his award speech, where he let the world know his inspiration.

The song was a ballad, so different from most of their music. Simple in its melody, with the lyrics doing all the heavy lifting. It was almost more poetry than music, the words telling the story of our childhood living next door to each other from a slightly different perspective than my own but filled with the same tension and want I had always thought was my experience alone.

I realized while listening to his words that this was real. Not that I hadn't believed him earlier when he'd told me he'd had feelings for me in the past, but this put a face on it. A million different emotions washed through me as the song drew on. It was such a beautiful and personal piece; it seemed too intimate for a rock band that sold itself on noise and sex. But at the same time, it fit. It fit Carter's voice perfectly, and it fit what I knew of him, both as a boy and now as this grown-up version of himself.

The last chords faded away into the night, and there was a stillness. Six thousand people sat in complete silence for a full heartbeat before the applause started. The feelings overwhelming me made it difficult to focus on Carter when he finally turned from the piano to thank the crowd and say good night. Our eyes locked for a split second before he walked off the stage, and I knew he had seen how moved I was by the words he wrote.

The crowd started to file out of the venue when the lights came up a moment later, breaking the spell for the thousands who got to leave and resume their normal lives. People rushing to catch trains, to drive back to their suburban homes, or to tell coworkers about the show the next morning around the water cooler. For me it would never be that easy.

I waited for a good ten minutes in my seat. I was grateful I had the time before someone came to get me, as I was feeling a little shaky on my feet, and I wasn't sure whether I could walk in a straight line fast enough to follow. Cory (or Cody) brought me back to Carter's dressing room. I thanked him and did a quick wipe of my face to make sure there were no residual signs of my emotional reaction to the final song. Before I could knock on the door, it swung open, and Carter was once again standing in front of me.

"I thought I heard voices out here," he said, before I could stutter out a greeting.

"Just me," I responded awkwardly and obviously as he stepped to the side to let me in and shut the door behind him.

We were standing closer than before, neither of us making a move to separate.

"So what did you think?" he whispered, with far less confidence than he had shown moments ago in front of the crowd.

"You were… amazing," I breathed back, struggling to find the words to express how his performance had changed so much I thought I knew to be true.

We were like magnets, inexplicably pulled together. Unconsciously shifting our weight from one leg to the other so we seemed to draw closer with every passing moment.

"Yeah?" He smiled at me shyly.

He was near enough now that I felt his body heat radiating against me. We stared at each other. I barely wanted to blink in case I missed a second. He raised his right hand slowly, as if to give me a chance to stop him. My breathing was labored, lungs working in overdrive even though we were standing still. The back of his fingers grazed my cheek softly. I leaned into his touch, trying to imprint this moment forever in my brain.

He took the last step to close the distance between us, sliding the string-calloused fingers of his other hand along the back of mine, linking our fingers together.

"Chase," he whispered as his right hand cupped my cheek and he looked questioningly at me.

I whimpered quietly, unable to find any words as his mouth finally reached for mine. My mind went blank when he kissed me gently. His lips were impossibly tender, his movements slow and encouraging, and I could barely do more than breathe him in. His left thumb made leisurely circles over the back of my hand, his hand on my face holding me steady while he took me apart piece by piece with his soft lips. It was unquestionably the most sensual moment of my life.

"Chase," he said again against my mouth, breaking the kiss.

He carefully pulled back, long before I was ready for him to, searching my eyes for any sort of clue as to whether he had read me right or not. I swallowed, and we both stepped back a half step, smiling shyly at each other.

No, he hadn't read me wrong at all.

Carter

I COULDN'T wipe the stupid grin off my face. Nothing in my life had ever felt as right as kissing Chase. Call it selfish, but even with the thousands of people in the audience tonight, his approval was all I cared about.

Banging on my dressing-room door made us both jump and broke the spell we were under.

"Carter, you still in there? Gotta be out in ten!" Cory shouted through the door.

"Okay!" I called back.

I inhaled deeply, not wanting to go back to real life.

"Are you hungry? Can I take you to dinner so we can talk?" I asked, far more nervous than I should have been considering he already let me kiss him just a moment ago.

He nodded. "Yeah, I could eat."

I quickly grabbed the last of my crap, knowing that if I forgot anything, I could get it at the show tomorrow night.

It was unusual and a privilege to be playing back-to-back shows at the same venue. And the luxury of a real bed in a hotel tonight, instead of my cramped bunk on the tour bus, was something I had been looking forward to all day.

"Core, we're out of here," I called down the hall in the general direction of the Green Room as we walked away.

We headed to the exit, the massive stage-door security guard on my tail until we safely jumped into the waiting town car.

"Thanks again!" Chase called to him as he closed the door and waved.

"What was that about?" I chuckled. "Making friends with security?"

"Oh, I met him before the show. He was the one that let me in and brought me backstage. I named him Barracuda." He snickered.

"Yeah, that's about right," I agreed.

I gave the driver the address of my favorite burger joint. Far enough from the venue that we wouldn't get stuck in the same place as the postconcert crowd. Somewhere private enough that Chase and I could actually talk without being interrupted by fans every five seconds looking to get a photo with me. I normally didn't mind meeting people after the show; the fans buying albums and tickets were the reason why I got to play my guitar for a living, and I liked to remember that. But tonight I wanted to be alone with this perfect, adorable guy who I couldn't believe was here with me.

We pulled up to the diner and got seated in a semicircular red vinyl booth at the back, secluded enough from the handful of other diners so it felt like we could still have a private conversation. We both slid into the center, sitting close enough that our legs almost touched under the table despite the booth being designed to accommodate more people than only the two of us. We made small talk until the waitress took our orders, and honestly, even something as mundane as listening to him talk about the weather or commenting on how horrible the wallpaper was made me incredibly happy.

Chase told me about his life while we waited for our food. His crazy friends Ty and Graham, how much he loved his classes, one of the grad students he went to school with. Jealousy pinged in me from the way he talked about some guy named Eli with such admiration. I got the sense there were feelings there, but I tried not to dwell on it.

He'd had his own life for the past few years. I had no claim on him, and as much as I didn't like it, I was sure there would have been guys lucky enough to have earned his attention in his past. Just because I had lived almost like a monk, single-handedly debunking every stereotype about musicians sleeping with different groupies in each city, didn't mean he hadn't been with other people.

He talked through half of his burger, and my attention was equally fixed on his words and on the drip of mayo he had missed at the corner of his mouth. He paused halfway through a sentence to follow my gaze.

"What?" Chase said self-consciously.

"Nothing," I managed to squeak out in response.

He poked his tongue out a second later to lick away the errant drop of sauce. Call me pathetic, or just hard up, but that three-second move of his tongue made the blood rush to my cock embarrassingly quickly. I gawked at him, slack-jawed. He smirked knowingly at me, and at least I had the good grace to blush a little.

Our attention was drawn back to our meals. He asked me about me—life on the road and outside of my job. It was always tough to be 100 percent sure these days with even the closest friends what their motivation was for spending time with me. An ill-timed photo or a misinterpreted joke posted on social media or sold to an entertainment rag had been the downfall of some amazing public figures. I liked to think that I chose my circle wisely, but I had had a couple of close run-ins nonetheless. As public as my life was, it could also be incredibly lonely. But Chase simply wanted to get to know me. Not any random faceless famous musician, not even Carter West from Inevitable Thorns, but just Carter.

We joked and reminisced about the old times long after our food was gone. He was starting to look a little drained, and I was definitely feeling the exhaustion of tonight, and five straight months of touring, catching up with me. I settled the check, and he thanked me far too much for the few dollars his meal cost. My bank account was filled with more money than I knew what to do with, and buying him a simple hamburger brought me more joy than just about anything I had purchased with my newly earned money.

We got back into the car, and my heart ached knowing that our time was coming to an end. He gave the driver directions to his apartment building, and we made our way through the late-night traffic down to the Lower East Side. We were both quiet, not knowing what to say to each other after the conversation had seemed to flow so easily all evening.

The car came to a stop outside a decent-looking older brick low-rise, and we both got out. I wasn't angling for an invite up or anything else to happen between us tonight. I only wanted to make sure he got home safely and I got a chance to say good night. We both exited the car. I stuffed my hands in my pockets to fight the urge to touch him.

"Well, this is me." He laughed nervously, stating the obvious. "It was so good to see you, C," he said.

"Chase, I…." I paused, gathering the words I prayed would be enough to convince him to continue whatever sort of relationship we might have. "I want to keep talking to you, seeing you. Tonight was… perfect in every way. I know we're just getting to know each other again, and that I hurt you. But I don't want this to be one night and then we go our separate ways."

"I don't want that either," he agreed, though his tone was cautious. "Honestly, I'm not sure I can handle having a long-distance boyf—someone." He stumbled adorably, clearly not ready yet to assume the label I wanted so much to be real. But he had wanted to say it. That was promising, wasn't it?

I nodded to show my enthusiasm for the positive response he'd nearly awarded me.

"Let's go slow," I agreed. "I've got another three weeks on the road, and then we're on break for a month before we start the next album. We can talk and text, catch up on the time we've lost. And when I'm back, we'll see what this is."

"Okay," he said. A smile tugged at the corners of his lips.

I beamed, overjoyed that we were on the same page and I had bought myself time to deserve a full second chance.

"Okay," I echoed.

I moved in slowly to embrace him. He fit so perfectly in my arms. His hair smelled like apples and cinnamon. I tried to memorize his scent and the feel of him against me for the long three weeks ahead. I kissed his cheek lightly, once, just a brush of my lips against his skin.

"Good night, Chase," I said as I stepped backward to the car.

He ducked his head but gave me a shy smile. "Night, C. Happy dreams."

Chase

THE day following the concert, I had a full calendar at school and then a music lesson for one of my students in the evening. By the time I was done, Carter was already into his second concert in New York, and their bus was scheduled to leave right after. It sucked that even with him in the city, we couldn't see each other.

The next few days passed slowly, and we were texting almost constantly. Any time that I wasn't in class and he wasn't in sound check or doing a show, it seemed like the messages were flying back and forth. We talked about anything that came to our minds: what was happening during the day, movies we had seen lately, our families. Carter's parents were still in Massachusetts, where they'd moved when we were in high school. His dad was career military and terrified of mandatory retirement in less than a year. His younger sister was a junior in high school, a softball player, the quintessential jock that his parents had always wanted him to be.

I filled him in on my family too; my much older parents were long since retired and were enjoying their house and surrounding large property. I told him about my older brother's success in his craft brewery and my cousins, who were always around when we were younger, and their latest feats.

We talked about his tour and the antics the band got up to and my classes and career aspirations. We talked about music. New bands we were into. Old songs we loved and had rediscovered.

We grew up playing music together. My dad always had a guitar around, and old-school rock 'n' roll records were forever on repeat in the background at my house. I think we were about six or so when we jointly approached our parents, begging for music lessons, dreaming of the band we would someday form together. While we both started lessons the next fall, Carter always leaned more toward plucking out single-note versions of 80s hair-rock songs on his guitar, while I leaped ahead on the piano, my teachers barely able to keep up with my appetite to learn. I started writing songs as soon as I knew enough notes to make a tune, the complexity of my melodies growing with my skills.

Carter's passion for heavier music and rock and my love for softer ballads and pop songs frustrated both of us whenever we got the semiregular idea to try forming a band again. We eventually conceded artistic differences around the beginning of high school but kept supporting each other in our own individual musical pursuits.

When Carter had to get a fake ID to get into the dirty club where he played his first gig just before we turned sixteen, I was right there with him, getting my own ID to watch the show. When I opened my acceptance letter to the acclaimed Julliard summer music school when I was fifteen, a letter that would eventually catapult me into attending the program I was in now, Carter was sitting beside me on my bed, handing me the letter opener.

It was no coincidence we were both in the music industry; it had been a lifelong passion for both of us, grown out of our friendship.

Since Carter had been away, we'd kept the flirting to a minimum over text. I think we were both hesitant to go too far down that road. But our attraction to each other was always just under the surface. I had mentioned a couple of times how much I liked the stubble he'd rocked when I saw him and, with a little prodding, had admitted how much his gravelly singing voice did it for me in that first number of his concert. He was sweet to me, giving me compliments at every turn that made my pale skin redden and my stomach fill with butterflies.

A few times he said good night with kissy emojis that left me warm and unable to sleep for hours afterward, thinking back to how good it had felt to have him kiss me in his dressing room. I was under no illusion that friendship was all he was looking for, and as much as my heart was ready to leap right in with him, my head held me back.

This was the same boy I had loved since my earliest memories. The boy who had utterly broken my heart when I finally worked up the courage to kiss him before he moved away. The boy who called me a word out of hate, a word that I can never remember him calling anyone else, even in his most heated arguments. The boy who ran out of my life after I poured my heart out to him and left me alone for five years.

Like it or not, that was our past, and while I finally understood his reason for lashing out at me that day, I was still working my way toward completely forgiving him. I knew we would get there, though. But that was only the short-term excuse I had for not jumping into this thing between us feet first. The bigger issue was his lifestyle and the amount of travel that would always be necessary in his job. That was the more permanent hurdle I wasn't sure I could get around.

Carter

LESS than a week left on tour and I was bouncing off the walls. I was so ready to be done with the whole thing. Ready to have my own space, my own bed. Hell, I couldn't even wait to get back to my own kitchen! I hated cooking, avoided it by whatever means necessary, but the thought of eating when I wanted and throwing some nice steaks on my own grill by this time next week? Sign me up.

Most of all, I missed the fuck out of my guy. I had no idea how, but the two weeks we had been apart felt longer than the five years separating us originally. I didn't know how things were going to go between us, but if I had any say in the matter, I knew what I wanted to happen.

Our schedules finally lined up, and we had plans to skype tonight after the show. We were playing our last back-to-back shows at the same venue this weekend, which meant we wouldn't have to overnight in the bus, so I was going to call him from my hotel room when I got there.

Sound check passed uneventfully, but there was a holdup for a tripped fire alarm when the house was loading in, so the start of the show was delayed. I'm sure I pissed off every member of our touring crew and my bandmates alike asking every five minutes what the status was, like a child on a road trip incessantly wondering if we were there yet. Finally the opening band took the stage, and I texted Chase to let him know I was going to be later than I planned, but things were progressing. The rest of the show carried on without incident, and the second it was over, I hightailed it out to my waiting car.

I hopped in the shower when I was in the hotel room, taking longer than I intended, unable to resist the luxury of even-temperature water washing over me after a solid two weeks of scrubbing down hastily in horrible theater basement shower facilities. Once I was clean, I threw on some comfy pajama bottoms and a loose charcoal T-shirt and crawled under the covers in the massive king bed with my laptop resting on my legs. I let Chase know I was ready when he was and fucked around on social media for five minutes while I waited for him.

The distinct ringing sound was loud in the quiet room and made me jump, but I quickly settled and connected the call. His beautiful face appeared on my screen, and he looked just as good as he had that night two weeks ago.

"Hey, baby," I said, the endearment slipping unconsciously from my tongue.

He smiled to himself, not seeming to have a problem with it, so I took that as a good sign.

"Hey, C. How did the show go?"

I proceeded to fill him in on the fire alarm and the rest of the evening, reveling in the fact that I actually got to see his face, his expressions and reactions, filling my screen. He told me about his day—a funny story about one of the kids he was teaching beginner lessons to, and a paper that he'd gotten a better mark than he had expected on. With all the daily stuff gone through, we both paused for a second, laughing at the same time and enjoying getting to see one another. God, I missed him.

"So, um, I've been thinking about you. A lot," he said, his cheeks and ears taking on a rosy blush.

"Oh yeah?" I flirted back, not sure where he was going with this but more than happy to hear his words, however they were meant.

"I can't stop thinking about when you kissed me."

I caught my breath quietly. I would have been happy with whatever direction his thoughts about me took; just knowing he was thinking about me in any context was more than enough to keep me smiling. But to hear he was thinking about me in that light made me feel amazing.

"Me too, baby. I've wanted to do that for so long." I wasn't sure how much I should admit to, but neither did I want to pass up the opportunity to see how much he would elaborate.

"I guess I always thought about it, what it would be like. And then you kissed me, and it was nothing like how I imagined it would be, and now I can't stop thinking about that," he blurted out adorably.

"How was it different?" I asked, genuinely curious.

"Softer," he whispered. "Slower. More intimate." He closed his eyes for a brief second, touching his lower lip as if inviting the memory. "I dunno. Is that… lame to say?"

I fought back a groan at his description of our kiss, immediately aroused by his breathy tone and how turned on he appeared to be. I squirmed a little, my dick showing interest and pressing uncomfortably against my laptop through the covers.

"Not at all." I shook my head, swallowing hard. "I want you to know how important this... you... are to me. I want you to know how special you are. How much you deserve to be cherished."

I paused, suddenly scared I had said too much or come on too strong.

"Unless.... You don't want it to just be... physical? Do you?" I hesitated, knowing I wanted so much more from him and terrified for a second I had completely misread the situation.

"No!" He blurted it out quickly, his ears growing even more red, endearingly, from his sudden outburst. "It's just... just more feelings involved from the beginning than I expected. And that's scary because I don't know what we are, or what we can be. We have too much history for me to be okay having casual sex with you, but I've never really had a serious relationship before, so I don't know how to do more than casual either."

I paused for a second. "Can I be honest with you, Chase?" I said, gentling my approach a little, ready to lay everything on the line with him.

"Always," he said without hesitation.

"Chances are you're more experienced with this stuff than I am. I have absolutely no idea what I'm doing here. I've already hurt you once, and anything that might hurt you again isn't a risk I'm willing to take." I hoped he understood what I was getting at without my actually having to say the embarrassing words.

"What do you mean? Like, you've never had a boyfriend?" he asked, clearly not catching the wavelength I was trying to send him.

"Well, technically no to that too. But I mean, I've never really, um.... I was young and closeted and scared to death of men and myself, and by the time I wasn't afraid anymore, enough people knew my name and face that I couldn't go to a bar anonymously and pick someone up. So I just... never did." I released the breath I didn't know I was holding.

I left out the part about how I had been in love with him since I was a teenager and was convinced that no man could compare to how I imagined him to be in bed—or as a boyfriend in general. Besides that little omission, everything I told him was the simple truth.

I had often thought there was such a weird hang-up in our society about virginity being both something you should get rid of quickly and also something that you should hold on to as long as possible. A damned if you do, damned if you don't scenario. That was a large part of the reason I had never been with anyone. I was afraid of being judged for not knowing what to do and admitting I was still a virgin at my age, especially since everyone assumed that because I was a musician, I was getting laid in every city I went to. The truth was, aside from a few chaste stolen kisses, I was as inexperienced as they came.

"Wait, what?" He looked more surprised than judgmental.

"This is all new to me. Relationships. Sex. Everything," I said quietly.

He paused, processing.

"That's okay." His voice was soft and reassuring. "There's nothing wrong with that. I just... didn't expect it."

I breathed a silent sigh of relief. I'd trusted him not to make a big thing out of my lack of experience, but his simple acceptance told me even more definitively how kind and open-minded he was.

"Are you opposed to...?" he asked, half joking, eyebrows raised, after a moment of silence.

I chuckled, letting the last of the tension drop from my shoulders. I was relieved, but not surprised, it was so easy to talk to Chase about something I would never dare to bring up with anyone else.

"With you? God, no. Chase, I want you so badly."

He made a sound somewhere between a contented sigh and a sexy moan my cock really, really liked, bringing it quickly back to life.

"What would you want to do with me first?" Chase said on a breathy exhale.

He adjusted himself subtly on his bed, getting comfortable. Oh hell yes. I was completely on board with this.

"I'm desperate to kiss you again," I admitted. "I want to find out your favorite way to be kissed. What you like. What… what makes you hard."

Chase bit his bottom lip, his eyes closed. I doubt he was even aware he was doing it. He was so damn sexy, without even trying. His reaction motivated me to keep going. We had never really discussed sex as teenagers, which had been a conscious decision on my part. Easier to avoid the subject than risk him finding out he was the object of all my fantasies. But this didn't feel unnatural, talking about it now. Quite the opposite, actually. It felt completely right, so I kept going.

"I want to feel your tongue in my mouth, to kiss you until you start to pant and beg me to go faster."

His face was getting more and more relaxed. His arms were out of the frame, but the camera on the computer balanced on his legs started rocking a little. God, the thought of him touching himself, being that turned on by my words, had me reaching down to join him in giving myself some much-needed relief.

"I want to taste your body. I'd pull off your shirt and kiss you everywhere I could reach. I want to know where you're sensitive. Want to touch you where you come unglued and where you… can't help but moan. Want to feel all of your skin under my tongue. Make you feel so good."

It was becoming more of a challenge to keep my voice even. The soft noises Chase was making were exquisite, and the feeling of my hand on my cock was making it difficult to think. His camera went crooked for a second, and then the angle changed so it was scrolling down his naked chest. I had a good idea about his intended destination for that camera.

"Wait!" I exclaimed.

The screen shot back up, and his expression went from bliss to fear in a split second. I hastily tried to reassure him that I didn't want to stop.

"Can I… can you leave it on your face? I want to see you touch yourself so badly, but the first time I… I want to see your face." I blushed, certain that it was a stupid and embarrassing request that would scare him off.

The fact was, knowing this was him was what was doing it for me. Seeing how *he* was reacting to me, seeing *his* face contorted in pleasure—that was turning me on so much. I wanted to watch Chase's expression when he came more than I wanted my next breath.

He whimpered, nodding, the muscles in his face easing once more.

"Yeah. That's really… yeah. I wanna see you too."

His eyes were a little unfocused now as he went back to pleasuring himself. His breathing became ragged, and the sexy-as-fuck sounds he was making grew more desperate, making me stroke myself faster in response.

"Fuck, C. Love seeing you like this. So fucking hot. Thought about you like this so much."

His dirty words rocketed me closer to my climax. While I had never in my life gotten off with another person, I was fairly confident it was supposed to last longer than this, especially since we couldn't actually touch each other. "Want to touch you so bad, Chase. God, baby. I'm so close. Please tell me you are too."

"So close," he babbled over and over, like the sexiest prayer I'd ever heard.

I was going to come any second. My cock was leaking like crazy, my balls tight and high. My whole body was coiled and tense.

"Fuck!" he shouted finally, his small frame trembling in release.

The incredible look on his face rocking in spasm sent me hurtling over the edge a second behind him. "Fuck, fuck, fuck!" I echoed, my body rolling through the most intense orgasm of my life.

We both lay there for a good minute or so. My speeding pulse evened out, and Chase's breathing slowed to something closer to normal, coming down from the crazy high we'd just shared.

And then the giggles started. His face broke into laughter, and he quickly covered his mouth with his—unused—hand.

"What?" I asked, laughing as well, unable to deny this man anything and finding every single thing about him utterly perfect.

"I never in a million years thought that would happen." He smiled so wide I thought my heart would break.

"Me neither," I replied, aching to touch him more than anything and knowing that I had just fallen even harder for my best friend.

Chase

THE three-week countdown was reduced to days and then hours. I tried any method available to distract me from our upcoming reunion, anticipating the full month we'd have together after his tour ended. After our... eventful Skype date, the time until I saw him was at least manageable, and I threw myself into my schoolwork for the last few days of our separation.

We kept texting like we had been doing since he left, but it took on a racier tone now. His tour schedule left him traveling on the bus nightly for the rest of their dates, so unfortunately we didn't get to have a repeat of our Skype fun, leaving us both frustrated and even more eager to see each other.

On the day before Carter was due back in town, my classes ended relatively early. I caught up with Eli, my former TA turned sort of friend, as he was leaving one of the studios at the same time I was getting out of my last class.

"Hey, teach," I called out to him when I was close enough for him to hear me.

Eli was somewhat of a rising star in classical piano circles, attracting the attention of the Artistic Director of the New York Philharmonic early in the master's program Eli had now almost completed. I had so much respect for his musicianship, and he was my go-to person for career-related advice these days.

Eli and I had a solid relationship. I may have misinterpreted his kindness in our early days and had a bit of a hopeless crush on him last year, right when he was starting to date his boyfriend, Ryan. Eli and Ryan were the definition of an up-and-coming power couple in the New York arts scene. Ryan worked as an administrator for a major theater company, and his brilliance at planning and logistics balanced out Eli's creativity to a tee. It wasn't until I saw them together that I understood they were made for each other and I had absolutely no chance with Eli. Eli had fallen fast, and no other guy would ever be on his radar. Now we were friends, and the awkwardness of my infatuation was basically forgotten.

He greeted me with a brief hug. "Hey! I haven't seen you around much lately."

"I've been around. Busy. Classes. The usual," I replied, shrugging.

"Yeah, that tends to happen in junior year. Wanna grab a coffee really fast? I have office hours in half an hour, so I've gotta make it quick."

I nodded, and we headed in the direction of the closest coffee shop on campus, filling each other in on pieces we were working on and program gossip.

"So how's Ry?" I asked when we were seated with our steaming mugs in front of us.

"He's fine. They're in casting for a new off-Broadway musical right now, so he comes home each night with some crazy stories of failed auditions. He's stressed out by the whole process, but that's nothing new. What about you? Any new guys hanging around?" He raised his eyebrows suggestively at me.

Carter and I were so new and undefined, I hesitated, not sure if he would want me broadcasting whatever was happening between us.

"There's… a guy," I started.

Eli is a good listener, and I was still conflicted about the whole situation with Carter. Maybe an outside perspective would help me get a grip on how I felt and what I wanted. A grin broke out on Eli's face.

"A guy is good. Tell me more." He sat back, ready for me to go on.

"It's… complicated. I knew him a million years ago, and we were close. I had a wicked crush on him forever, but he was in the closet. I made a move right before his family left town when we were in high school, but it didn't go over very well, and we hadn't spoken since. But now we've… reconnected, and it's good between us. Really good. His job is high-profile. He's out now, but he's gone a lot. All my feelings are coming back super quickly, and I just don't want to fall for him and then for him to leave again."

I dumped everything on him, talking way too fast and realizing how good it felt to get it off my chest.

Eli took a minute to think before he responded to my rambling dialogue. "Wow, that is a lot. And he feels the same way you do now?"

"I think so. He admitted recently he had feelings for me back then too, but he wasn't ready to come out." I omitted exactly how public the declaration of his feelings for me had been. "We've been texting and flirting while he's been gone the past month, and it's gotten… intense." *To say the least*, I added in my head. "He gets back tomorrow, and we've been talking about seeing each other a lot while he's around. Seeing what happens."

Eli nodded. "I guess it all boils down to two questions. Is taking the risk on him worth it, and is being with him sometimes enough to make up for when he's gone."

Eli was full of all kinds of crazy insight. What he said made sense. I only wished I knew for sure what the answer was.

"And how good the sex is," Eli tacked on with a wink, as if to disprove my inflated opinion of his maturity. I snorted at his crassness.

"You're right. I just don't know what I want." I couldn't help a little bit of dejection in my voice.

"You don't have to decide today. Take some time. Get to know him again and see what you want. You don't owe him anything. Put yourself first, and do what's right for you."

I nodded, thinking back to how Ty had basically given me the same advice.

"Yeah. It's just, when he's around, I can't think straight. He's gorgeous. Charming. We connect about music. Have the same sense of humor. His voice, the way he looks at me…. He's completely overwhelming, in the best possible way."

Eli chuckled at my doe-eyed description. "Well, that says a lot too. The best ones are completely distracting. Talk to him. See where he's at. Maybe he's willing to make changes to be with you too. He sounds like someone worth fighting for." Eli's face took on a longing expression. Clearly thoughts of his own man were running through his mind.

I agreed with him. It was useful advice, even though I couldn't tell him the specifics and I was skeptical about how much Carter would ever be able to change his travel situation.

Eli glanced at the clock on the wall behind me, taking the last sip of his coffee. "Well, I should go. Let me know what happens with your guy. You're smart. You'll figure it out."

He stood, offering me a hug and a farewell before he walked out the door and back to his office. I made my way downtown, stopping to pick up some Thai takeout for an early dinner before I got home. The weekend was in front of me and Carter's visit at the forefront of my mind.

Carter

I STEPPED through the automatic doors to the airport with the one duffel bag of clothes that weren't shipped home and the acoustic guitar I never traveled without. I made sure my sunglasses were on and pulled my ballcap down a little to shadow my face. Going through DC wasn't nearly as bad as flying through LAX, but there were wannabe paparazzi with camera phones everywhere.

I breezed through check-in, looked at the time on my smartphone, and made my way to a secluded corner near my gate. I scrolled through my messages, with only one new one from Chase telling me he was on his way home from school to start his weekend, and he was looking forward to seeing me tomorrow. Little did he know, I had sweet-talked my manager into changing my ticket for a day earlier than the rest of the band,

and I would be at his door in only a couple of hours. I smiled to myself, unable to contain my elation.

I made my way through JFK like I had done it a million times. Maybe it hadn't been quite a million, but it had been enough that I knew the layout and where the washrooms were. I ducked into a restroom to freshen up a little. It didn't help a lot, but it was the best I could do right now, and I was too enthusiastic to get to Chase's apartment to spend much time cleaning up. I hopped in a cab, giving the driver the same address Chase provided the night of the NYC concert. We slowly made our way through the freeways and then across the grid of lower Manhattan, inching my way closer to having Chase in my arms again.

I texted Cory, letting him know I'd made it, and then sent a few quick replies to messages from fans on my social media accounts. I refrained from texting Chase, not trusting myself to avoid inadvertently blurting out my plan and ruining the surprise five minutes before I showed up.

We arrived in front of his building. I paid the driver and gave him a generous tip for getting me to Chase's quickly before I pulled my bag and guitar out of the trunk. With the attempted disguise no longer required, I took off my hat and sunglasses. I wanted nothing more than for my guy to see my face when I got to his apartment.

A delivery driver was fortunately exiting the building when I got to the doors, so I let myself in. I headed to the elevator, buzzing with nervousness as much as excitement. The elevator was slow to arrive and slower to get to his floor.

I walked quickly down the hall, feeling like I had run a marathon by the time I located his door. Taking a calming breath, I ran a hand through my hair and knocked. Footsteps grew louder, the lock clicked, and then the door swung open.

I had never in my life seen anyone look more beautiful. He was wearing a pair of blue flannel pajama pants and an oversized hunter green Julliard sweatshirt, grown soft and ragged from wear. His feet were bare, and his hair was a little bit of a mess, still damp from a recent shower. But to me, he had never been so handsome.

He was blocking the doorway, obviously completely shocked to see me. His hands went to pull at his clothes self-consciously while he struggled to find the words to greet me. So I jumped in and spoke first.

"I couldn't wait until tomorrow," I said simply, with a shrug and a guilty smile.

And all at once, he shrieked and pounced on me. I had only a second to drop my guitar case to make sure I could catch his weight. Nothing on the planet had ever made me show such little regard for my treasured instrument, but in that moment, it was merely something else keeping me from holding Chase the way I wanted to. He wrapped his legs around my hips and glued himself to my chest. His arms went around my back, hugging me so tightly I was mildly concerned about damage to my ribs. I drank him in. The smell of his apple shampoo as I buried my nose in his hair. The perfection of his weight in my arms. The feeling of him as he enthusiastically kissed my neck, my jaw, anything he could reach, was exquisite. I wanted to live in that moment forever.

Just when I thought it couldn't possibly get any better, his lips found mine in a brutal, possessive kiss. This kiss was nothing like the first time. It was aggressive and determined and passionate. Weeks, months, years of desire channeled into one unbelievably hot meeting of our lips.

His tongue demanded entrance to my mouth, rolling and sucking until I was achingly hard and a wobbly pile of goo all at the same time. I grabbed his thighs, steadying him while he squirmed against me. My arms burned from holding him up, keeping him both safe and as physically close to me as humanly possible.

I had the fleeting thought that we were standing in his doorway, wide open for anyone walking by in the hallway to see us. Even though we were in the heart of the East Village, the gay mecca of New York City, there was still such a thing as common decency. I bent slightly to lift my guitar case and bag with one hand, never breaking our kiss, carried him into the apartment, and slammed the door behind me.

"Oh God, C," he moaned against my mouth once we were inside.

My arms were melting into jelly because he was turning me on so much. I gently encouraged him to stand on his own.

"What are you doing here?" he gasped, barely detaching himself from our embrace.

"I couldn't wait," I said again. "Caught… an earlier flight." I barely managed to get the words out between kisses.

He pinned my back against the door. The urgency of the kiss was fading, but it was still intense and demanding. His hands framed my face, controlling the kiss and holding me where he wanted me. His hips were tight against mine; the pressure of his hard cock aligning with my own was making me lose my mind. I could already feel the heat radiating through his thin pajama pants. I found the perfect globes of his ass and clutched him tighter against me, encouraging him to roll his hips into me. We were moaning and gasping into each other's mouths. I had no idea how I knew what to do. Instinct, I guess, or the few gay porn videos I had seen in desperate moments when nothing else would satisfy my horniness.

"Bed," he finally demanded, breaking the kiss for a fraction of a second.

He pulled me farther into his small apartment, which was a feat in itself as we simply were not capable of taking our hands off each other. We had to stop several times on the short walk to make out, grabbing at each other to bring us closer together.

When we finally made it into his bedroom, he drew his mouth away from mine, breathing heavily. He stroked my cheek and looked at me deeply. His pupils were blown, his hair was all over the place, and his lips were red and swollen. He looked completely debauched and more beautiful than ever.

"Is this okay, C? We don't have to do this if you're not ready."

His care and consideration broke me. I nodded, needing to reassure him that I wanted this as much as he did. Maybe more.

"Maybe not... everything tonight. But God yes. I want this. Want you," I stammered, gasping for air between broken sentences.

He responded by kissing me again. Slower this time, but just as powerfully. He lifted his arms, and I gathered the hem of his shirt, running my fingers up his torso while I pulled it over his head. I explored his back, gliding my fingers up and down his spine while he caressed my jaw. The heat from his skin, the amazing feeling of his naked body under my hands, was overwhelming.

I moved to study the curvature of his chest while he slid my shirt over my head and took my hands off him for mere seconds as he slipped the unwanted garment off. Then I reached for him again. I ran my hands over his collarbone. I nuzzled his pecs, his flat stomach, his pretty pink nipples, which made him gasp. The reaction encouraged me to play with them some more, circling the pebbled skin until the buds grew hard under my fingers. The noises I was drawing from him were so fucking hot. I pressed my body against his. His breath was warm against my neck, and I locked my hips to his as I continued rolling and pinching the rosy nubs with my thumb and forefinger. He began gyrating his hips against mine, silently begging for friction on his still-clothed cock. A wet spot formed on the front of his pajama pants. Fuck, it was so hot how responsive he was.

"Stop, stop, or you'll make me come!" he finally cried out.

Hearing him say that skyrocketed me closer to my own orgasm.

I let go of his abused nipple and continued kissing his neck, slower this time. God, he felt so good. He leaned back a fraction, again questioning with his eyes as he slid his hands down my body, reaching for the button on my jeans. I nodded with maybe a little too much enthusiasm, biting my lip to prevent myself from crying out. After toeing off my boots to get them out of the way, I ran my fingers along his midriff, dipping them just inside the elastic of his pants to tease. The back of his hand skimmed my throbbing cock when he pulled down the zipper. I was so close already, it wasn't going to take much to set me off.

My jeans fell from my hips and landed in a pile at my feet. I kicked them away and dragged Chase's body back against mine as close as I could get him. There were still far too many clothes in the way. Hungrily kissing him, I slid his pants down over the silky-smooth skin of his ass, gripping and squeezing the taut muscles as they were revealed.

He guided me toward his bed and laid us down on our sides next to each other, fervidly touching and exploring. He looped his thumbs into my boxer briefs and pulled them down over my red, swollen length, finally leaving nothing between us. Seeing his cock exposed for the first time made my mouth water. He was perfectly proportioned, uncut, and dripping fountains from the dark head.

Our strenuous gasping made it difficult to maintain a kiss for any length of time. He ran his fingers down the underside of my cock, making me moan and shake with need. He rolled over, reached into the drawer of his nightstand, and coated his fingers from the tube of clear liquid he kept there. God, imagining him using that on his own, touching himself alone at night, made me crazy.

He fisted my erection first and then his own, rubbing the lube over both of us. His hard cock next to mine was a sensation I wasn't prepared for. I struggled to keep it together, rolling my hips instinctively and uncontrollably.

I clawed at his ass as he worked both of us. My nerve endings were all firing simultaneously as his hand moved faster and faster, my breaths getting more erratic and my body tensing. Our eyes were locked, fighting to stay open as though neither of us wanted to miss a second. We gasped into each other's mouths for air.

"Oh God, C!" Chase cried out, and he spilled hot come over both of us.

I followed him a heartbeat later on a helpless moan, the vision of his cock spurting against mine etched in my brain. The image of our combined releases, mixing together on our spent cocks in his hand, was enough to wrench one last tremor from me. His hand slowed to a stop. I inhaled deeply, trying to regain some control of my body.

He ghosted his lips across my jaw, mouth curling into a grin against me.

"Was that okay?" he whispered into my ear. It seemed he suddenly needed reassurance after having displayed such confidence through the entire encounter.

"It was… perfect." My voice cracked as I tried to express with mere words how life-changing doing that with him really was. How experiencing this with him for the first time was everything I could have wanted, and how it meant so much more to me than simply the joining of our bodies.

He grabbed some tissues and cleaned us up quickly, both of us utterly wrung out.

"Stay with me?" he asked with a shy smile. As if I could ever deny this man anything.

"Always." I tucked him against me until his breathing evened out in contented sleep.

Chase

I WOKE up the next morning with some gorgeous, strong arms around my waist and a hard cock poking me in the back. I couldn't remember the last time a guy had spent the night with me, so the novelty of this feeling was very welcome.

I shifted slightly so I could turn over and see his sleeping face. His features were completely relaxed—his eyelashes fanning delicately across his high cheekbones and his untamed hair cascading down the pillow behind him. I had never seen such a stunning vision.

I rolled over fully so I was lying with my head on his chest; his arms seemed unwilling to let go of their grip on me. His sleepy warmth and masculine scent were so enticing. I slowly started running my fingers up and down his body, memorizing him through touch. His chest was toned and sexy. He kept himself in shape, with definition in his pecs and shoulders but not overly built up. He had a light spattering of hair on his chest, enough to know it was natural and he wasn't vain enough to wax it. I had always been insanely attracted to a man's arms, and fuck if his weren't absolutely flawless. His biceps turned me on immediately, radiating strength and control. His forearms were powerful from years of playing his guitars. My thoughts immediately morphed to a dirty fantasy of him pleasuring himself, stroking his thick cock with all the muscles in his arms flexing and moving together to fuel his hand's frantic movements.

I made my way down his torso with my fingertips when he stirred, found a resting spot for my palm on his lickable hip bone, and made small circles over his smooth skin with my thumb.

"Mmm," he hummed, stirring against me. "Good morning, gorgeous." Carter's gravelly morning voice rumbled sweetly. "Did you sleep well?"

"So well," I said, gazing up at him from my position on his comfortable chest.

I continued grazing his skin with my thumb, moving closer and closer to his very awake cock. He purred his approval, his head back against the pillows.

I shifted my weight, sinking down his bigger body. I kissed him along his side as I moved farther south. His breathing hitched when he realized where this was going. I ran my fingers across his full balls, enjoying the feeling of their heavy weight in my hand. When I kissed his hip, he gasped at my light morning stubble abrading the sensitive skin there.

His quivering thighs opened for me, letting me sink my body between them. I leisurely stroked my way across his hip toward his cock, which was fully engorged, the skin tight and red and the vein running down it pulsing with want. His dick was the ideal size. Average length, from my admittedly limited firsthand experience, with a little additional girth for the perfect stretch when and if we ever took that next step. I buried my nose in the nest of soft curls that framed his cock, enjoying his musky scent. From the back of my throat, I made an involuntary noise of pleasure, getting off on this as much as he was.

I looked up at his beautiful face. His eyes were shut and his mouth slightly open, his expression one of pure bliss. He ran his hand through my hair gently, fingers entangled in the messy strands. I caressed his inner thighs, toying with the coarse hair and teasing closer and closer to his groin.

I mouthed around his throbbing length, increasing the anticipation by letting him feel the moisture from my breath. His panting was growing labored, the gasps and cries sounding needier with each second. After teasing us both to the point of insanity, I couldn't wait another second. I lightly swirled my tongue against the head of his cock, groaning into it as his flavor burst onto my taste buds. Fuck, he tasted so good.

"Holy shit!" Carter exclaimed, arching halfway into the air.

I chuckled. Holding his hips down against the mattress, I assaulted him with my mouth. I licked and sucked, pulling out every trick I knew to bring him the maximum amount of pleasure. The noises he was making were driving me wild. Fuck, I'd never had any man so turned on beneath me when I'd done this before. It was making me all sorts of confident in my rusty abilities, causing me to push aside my stubborn gag reflex and suck him into a vacuum as if my life depended upon it. I had forgotten how much I enjoyed doing this.

"Chase. Baby, fuck. Chase. Fuck!" He was nearly incoherent, grasping at my head, my shoulders, the bedsheets. Anything he could reach. "I'm gonna... oh fuck. I'm gonna. Oh God...." His whole body convulsed, and his come pulsed down my throat. I swallowed around him, drinking down every drop.

"Oh my fuck," he muttered to the ceiling when he was finally empty.

Carter's pulse worked overtime even as his body went slack with release. My cock was impossibly stiff between my legs. It would take no more than a stroke or two to finish it off after the unbelievably sexy show Carter had put on. He opened his eyes, and a lazy smile bloomed across his face.

"Come here," he said, grasping me.

I went to him willingly, straddled him and sat lightly on his chest. He reached for my aching shaft.

"Not… gonna… last," I managed to gasp when his hand closed around me.

He hummed in response. "Tell me how you like it," he said, starting to jerk me, his other hand on my ass to steady me.

"Faster…," I breathed. "Touch the head. Yes, like that!"

My body was writhing on top of his. Carter's grip on my cock tightened just enough, and he picked up the pace. He was way too good at this for never having had sex with a partner before. A second later, he started executing an impossibly good curved stroke at the top, hitting all the nerve endings in the crown. That was all it took to set me off. I cried out as my come erupted over his eager hand. He kept caressing me through it, drawing out my pleasure.

Never breaking eye contact, Carter slowly brought his come-covered hand to his mouth. He swirled his index finger between his lips, tasting my release. I groaned. If I hadn't just gotten off, that would have been enough on its own to send me over the edge.

"Come here," he said, bringing my head down to his for a scorching kiss, and we savored each other as our tongues met.

Chase

CARTER'S footsteps made their way down the short hall as I finished throwing pancakes and bacon onto both of our plates.

"This smells amazing, baby. Thank you," he mumbled against my neck, wrapping his arms around my waist from behind.

He kissed me in the goose-bumps-inducing spot behind my ear.

"Mmm," I sighed happily, but when he didn't stop kissing up and down my neck, I said, "Better eat them before they get cold."

He gave my earlobe one last nibble before letting me go, then pulled out two barstools from under the counter. We ate together in a companionable silence. Food had been the last thing on our minds the night before, and I hadn't realized how famished I was until I started stuffing my face.

"So what do you want to do with your first day off?" I asked him when we were clearing our plates into the sink.

"I was thinking I'd like to take you out on a date." His response came so fast, I suspected he had already been thinking about it before I asked. "What's your idea of a perfect date?"

I was a little stunned and couldn't form words at first. Nobody had ever asked me that before. The few dates I'd been on were some combination of drinks, dinner, or coffee, with the assumption that we would be going back to one or the other's place afterward. A date? With Carter? I had no idea what that would look like.

"Um…?" My brain wasn't functioning, and nothing jumped out at me immediately. "I don't know?"

"I was thinking about skating," he said, thankfully taking the pressure off me. "You know, like we used to do on the pond behind your parents' property when we were little?"

"That sounds… perfect." I was awed by his suggestion. A thoughtful idea and one that would remind us of our childhood. I was almost afraid to say anything more for fear of breaking the moment.

Carter gently stroked my chin between his thumb and index finger, lifting my face while he covered my mouth with his. "Perfect," he echoed against my lips.

We finished cleaning up after breakfast, working together seamlessly, stealing touches and kisses whenever we got close enough to make contact. I had never seen this sweet, tender side of him before. It made me even happier that we hadn't gotten together when we were kids, because I'm sure he wouldn't have been like this at sixteen, and I was a total sucker for romance.

Once the kitchen was taken care of, I had to start getting ready for the couple of music lessons I had to teach that afternoon. I thought about calling to cancel, work being the last thing I wanted to focus on today, but Carter encouraged me to keep the appointments. Most of the young students I tutored were only available on Saturdays, and they didn't deserve to fall behind because their teacher was finally getting some.

"Do what you have to. I'll check in with my place for a bit, maybe take a nap. I want to pick you up properly for our date tonight, make it everything you deserve. I want to make things easier for you, not disrupt your life," he said when I protested his leaving.

I wavered. "I could use the money...."

"Then it's sorted. Is four o'clock too early for me to come and get you?"

"Four is good." I smiled at him.

"Then it's a date." He bopped me on the nose lightly, making me giggle.

I opened the door for him, stretching to kiss him, his hands full of his bag and his guitar case. I let the kiss linger, both of us delaying being separated, even for a few hours.

"Have a good day, C. Welcome home."

"See you tonight, sweetheart," he said, already better at this than I was.

He pecked me once more and then sauntered down the hall toward the elevator.

Carter

I CRAWLED into my bed just after noon, hoping to grab a quick nap before I headed back to Chase's. The soft white linens on my bed were nothing like the cramped bunk on the bus, or even the hotel rooms I had made my home in recently. I was relaxed in a way I hadn't been in so long, but the two mind-blowing orgasms may have also contributed to that.

The heavy drapes that covered the floor-to-ceiling windows blocked out the light, making my room feel cozy and warm despite how bright the sunshine was on this cold March morning. It felt like I hadn't slept in months, which was true enough.

Life on tour was anything but opulent, and I wanted to sleep for about a week straight to make up for the pure physical exhaustion I felt. It probably hadn't helped that

Chase and I were up far later than we should have been last night. Not that I would have traded that for anything.

His suggestive words and the sounds he'd made were playing like an unending loop in my mind, leaving me in a constant state of arousal. I'd had no idea at all that it could be like that. I had never had an excessive sex drive; I mean, duh, nobody who sees sex as a consistent essential would have remained a virgin as long as I had. But man, could I see the appeal of getting laid on the regular after the past fourteen hours.

Not just laid, I corrected. The thought of casual sex made me even more queasy than it had before. What I'd shared with Chase last night—I couldn't imagine that ever being satisfying as something meaningless between strangers. No, it should be an intense connection with a partner. Someone I could explore for hours, learning every facet of his body and maximizing the ways to turn him on. And honestly, right now that someone had been narrowed down to one perfect man.

I wanted Chase. In every way that I could have him. However he chose to give himself to me. We hadn't gotten to the point yet where we needed to have a big sit-down about what we were to each other and where this was going, but I knew what I wanted, and I hoped he was looking for the same thing. It was so new, but it also felt like it had been twenty years in the making. I was not going to fuck it up a second time.

My mind wandered to future events with him. Us sitting cross-legged under the tree on our first Christmas together, opening gifts. Maybe he was wearing a Santa hat and some fluffy reindeer pajamas. Taking him to Paris and seeing him light up when he got a look at the Eiffel Tower for the first time. Watching him proudly when he walked across the stage to get his diploma from Julliard.

I finally drifted off, happier than I could remember being. The future was wide open with possibilities.

My alarm woke me a while later. My mind was fuzzy, and I could have slept for hours still. I made myself a quick sandwich from the fridge that I'd had stocked for me before I got home and turned on the TV to zone out with some crap cooking show. Soon enough, it was time to get ready.

I sent a quick text to Chase, asking how his lessons went and making sure the time we agreed on was still good for him. I was in the middle of tying my hair into a bun when my phone dinged with his response. It was a selfie that made my heart stop.

The top half of his head was peeking out from behind a shower curtain, his hair frothy with shampoo lather, the rest of him hidden in the shower.

Getting ready now! Cleaning all the important bits. He'd captioned the photo with a smiley face.

It was ridiculous. I couldn't see more than his bubbly blond hair, his emerald eyes, and half his nose, but it was the most erotic picture I'd ever seen in my life. Knowing he was naked and wet in the shower, his body hidden only by the light fabric drapery, turned me on so quickly I felt light-headed. My hair tie snapped painfully on my wrist from unconsciously overstretching it while my focus was on much more important matters.

"Ouch," I said, shaking my hand to try to lessen the sting.

I took a quick photo of myself naked from the waist up in the bathroom mirror. After pulling my hair back with one hand and purposely flexing a little more than I had to as payback, I sent it through quickly with a text saying *Getting ready too*, with a smirking emoji.

He responded immediately with an emoji of eyes popping out of his head and then followed up by texting *Well played*, with a face sticking out its tongue.

I mentally congratulated myself, laughing as I tied off my hair and spritzed a small amount of aftershave on my stubbled cheeks because I knew he liked the smell. Finishing up in the bathroom, I found a pair of jeans loose enough to skate in and paired them with a mint-green button-down with pale, shimmery vertical stripes and a long black wool coat from the back of my closet. I stepped into my worn boots, stuffed a pair of black leather gloves in my pocket, and headed for the door. A quick stop at a florist for a bouquet of vibrant lilacs and lavender and I was on my way to see my guy.

Chase

I OPENED my door for the second time in two days to Carter surprising the hell out of me. The first time, his presence alone had been a shock. This time he had flowers for me.

Nobody in my life had ever given me flowers. Growing up taking music lessons, we'd had a recital at the end of each year. All the girls always got bouquets from their families, but I never did. I remember being envious of their beautiful arrangements and being quietly disappointed every time I wasn't acknowledged in the same way.

But Carter had brought me lavender and lilacs, and I'm sure my face lit up for him like he'd given me the moon and the stars and the sun all at the same time.

I beamed, accepting the bouquet he held out to me. "You brought me flowers?"

"You always wanted some, remember? You told me that one year after your piano recital."

"I can't believe you remembered that. That must have been more than ten years ago," I said, astounded by his thoughtfulness.

"I remember everything about you, baby. And from tonight on, I want to make up all the time we lost and show you how much you mean to me."

I blushed and fought the sudden moisture in my eyes.

"I thought you started doing that last night." I had to sass him; his sincere words were too much for me to handle.

He chuckled. "Well, that too."

I put the beautiful blooms in a drinking glass in my kitchen with care, since I didn't even own a vase for them to go in. He took the opportunity when my hands were busy to wrap his arms around me and kiss me hello properly.

We headed off for Rockefeller Center before we got too carried away and skipped the date entirely. He got a couple of funny stares on the subway and the subsequent walk—that confused look of recognition but failure to place where from. I was disconcerted, but C was used to it, I guess, simply turning his head to talk to me or keeping his chin down so they couldn't see his features as clearly. For the most part it worked. He had worn his hair up too, his long locks being one of his most recognizable trademarks, so we were basically left alone until we got to the rink.

We made our way slowly through the line up to the skate-rental desk. The perky Miss Clairol number twelve blond twink behind the counter squeaked when we got to the front of the line, recognizing Carter immediately. Carter quickly leaned in over the counter. He slid the guy a healthy amount of money and whispered something to him sternly. The guy nodded, mimed zipping his lips, and turned to pick up two pairs of skates off the shelf, swapping them for our shoes.

We walked to the benches and sat side by side, and I asked Carter what the clerk had said.

"He knew who I was, and I didn't want to ruin our date. So I told him I would take a photo with him on our way out if he kept his trap shut for a couple of hours until we're done." Carter looked guilty. "I'm sorry, baby. I wanted today to be about us, but that's going to happen from time to time. Does it bother you?"

"No," I said truthfully. "I mean, does it ever get unsafe or uncomfortable for you?"

"For the most part it's okay, and I don't mind it. There's the occasional person who takes it too far and tries to grab me or something. I'm a big enough guy that I can generally keep control of the situation, but at shows there's security just in case. I hate when they come up to me at a restaurant or something and interrupt my meal."

I made a noise in acknowledgment.

"I keep my nose clean, so there's nothing too terrible they could find out about me. I get concerned sometimes that they'll eventually start bugging my family or people who didn't sign up for this life. Like you," he said, looking at me questioningly.

"You worry about me?" I asked as my heart melted a little.

"Of course I do, baby. Even before we were talking again, I worried about them digging up something about my childhood and somehow giving you a hard time. I would never want to do anything to make you unhappy or put you in danger."

He kissed my nose sweetly and pulled me up, my skates wobbling a little under me. It had been a long time since I had done this. I wondered how sore my ass was going to be after this little adventure. And not in the fun way.

"You ready to do this?" He raised his eyebrows.

"Absolutely." And giving my blades a test glide onto the rink, I accepted his challenge.

Carter

WE reluctantly gave up on the ice when we lost feeling in our toes from the cold. How was it still so cold by the middle of March in this city? We swapped our skates back for our shoes, and I kept my promise to the fan behind the counter. Chase glared at him the entire time. I wrapped my arm around Chase's waist when we were done with the photo.

"What's wrong, grumpy?" I teased, pulling an exaggerated pouty face to make him laugh.

"Nothing." He sounded a bit snappish but with no real force behind his words. It didn't take a genius to figure out what the problem was.

"Chase case, you know you're the only guy I've ever noticed and ever will, right?" I kissed his nose.

To me, it was so obvious it didn't need to be stated. I couldn't have cared less that Skater-twink Ken was obnoxiously flirting with me. There was no other man in the world worth flirting back with. Chase was the only one I wanted.

"How about I grab us some hot chocolate to warm up with, and we can talk?" I suggested gently.

"I don't need you to always buy me things. I can support myself," he said with a frown.

I was quick to reassure him. "I never said you couldn't. I asked you to come out with me, so I thought I should pay. But I'm new at this, and if that's not the way this works, that's fine too."

"You're right. I'm sorry. I'm just…. He was all over you, and—"

I cut him off with a kiss before his brain led him down a completely unnecessary road. "Hey. You, Chase Lucas Collins. Are. The. Only. Guy. I. Want," I said, and I kissed him in a different spot between each word.

He visibly fought the smile that crept up. "You probably shouldn't kiss me in public. Someone might see and take a photo or something."

"Let them." I shrugged. "There's nothing I would be prouder of than being seen with you." I cupped his face, kissing him properly.

"Fine," he said, the annoyance gone from his voice. "But I'll get the hot chocolate."

He came back a minute later with two steaming mugs. I found us a café table where we could sit and watch the other skaters while we sipped our treat. We sat in a contemplative silence for a moment, knowing there was more we needed to talk about, but both apparently reluctant to be the one to bring it up.

"C, I don't know…."

"Chase, I...." We both started at the same time and then laughed, some of the tension of the moment dissipating. I motioned for him to go ahead.

"I don't know what this is. I don't know what you want from me. I'm still wrapping my head around the fact that you're here, and you're gay, and you're, like, this well-known musician. But this thing between us— you look at me like you do and suddenly everything goes away. It feels too good to be true. I guess I'm just confused. You'll be gone so much, people know you, your life is far from private. I feel like there's something here, or there could be if you want it to be too, but every time I stop to think about it, there's another reason why this is a bad idea."

I took a long sip of my hot chocolate, buying myself a second to gather my words and pray I could articulate to him exactly how I felt.

"I get it, Chase. Completely. You have your own life, and I came in out of nowhere. My world isn't easy right now. In some ways, I've gotten a lot of what I've been trying to achieve for so long. But the touring, the lifestyle... it takes its toll on everyone. I'm not looking to make things more difficult for you. As much as I want to be with you, I want you to be happy even more.

"But I do want to be with you, Chase. For me, this isn't a new development. I've felt the same way about you since I was fourteen. I just finally have the balls to do something about it now. I want to be with you, Chase. I want to be your boyfriend. I want the late-night skyping and the morning pancakes, the skating dates. But I know you're the one that this will be a harder decision for. I want to prove to you that I can be worth the sacrifices. I want to do what I can to take on as much of the burden as possible. I will never consciously hurt you. I know it's worth it for me. I just need you to be sure it's worth it for you too."

He nodded slowly, absorbing every word I said.

"I want to be with you too," he finally said, his words slow and measured.

"But?" I asked, because it sounded like there was going to be a "but" there. I didn't want to give him the opportunity to retract what he had said, but I also wanted him to be 100 percent confident in his decision and not regret anything in a few weeks or months.

"No buts," he confirmed. "Well, I still want to work out what happens when you leave. But no buts. I want to be with you." He sounded more convinced this time.

The feeling in that moment was worth every self-conscious debate in my head, every hour of lost sleep before reaching out to him at the *Grammys*, every moment of panic when I didn't think he would respond to my desperate plea from the stage. A smile broke out on my carefully veiled face. I couldn't stop myself; I got out of my chair and moved around to his seat to kneel in front of him so we were on the same level. His eyes twinkled with mirth at my gesture. I caressed his handsome face and kissed his perfect lips thoroughly.

"Promise?" I asked against his lips.

"Promise," he whispered, kissing me again through our twin smiles.

Carter

MY original plan had been to take him to a fancy steak house at the top of one of the nearby skyscrapers, but we changed things up again and opted for a simpler meal of delivery pizza in my condo while watching a movie on the couch. I'm not going to lie, getting Chase alone was a much smarter idea, and I probably should have planned that from the beginning.

The credits were rolling, and I had a perfect, snuggly Chase lying with his head in my lap. I had been stroking his hair soothingly for the past hour at least, zoning out on the movie and focusing on how wonderful he was and how right this felt.

I would have thought he had drifted off if it wasn't for the occasional shift in his weight or happy sigh he gave.

He reached for the remote on the coffee table and clicked off the film, took my hand, and helped me up from the couch. I thought I had a good idea of where this was going, but he surprised me and led me into my adjoining music room instead of my bedroom.

"Will you play it for me again? My song?" he asked, kissing my hand when we were standing next to the baby grand piano.

"Always." I kissed the top of his head.

We sat down together on the bench like we had a million times when we were kids.

When we were about eleven, Chase and I had been obsessed with sharing an apartment in Manhattan when we grew up. We talked nonstop about having a studio to write and record music in our living room, with a glossy black Steinway in the corner for him and a wall of colorful Fender guitars for me. His piano—I always thought of it as his—was the first major purchase I made for myself when we signed with our record label. I remember having it picked out for months before all the paperwork with the label was done and I could finally afford it. I was still working on slowly acquiring the wall of guitars, but his piano made this place my home.

I ran my fingers over the underused keys, then started to play the song almost like I was in a trance, singing the melody softly into the quiet room. At one point, his arm snaked around my waist and his head found my shoulder while he listened to me play. I had performed for other people hundreds of times in my life. From piano recitals in elementary school to massive auditions for major record producers to busking on street corners to pay rent to concert venues throughout the US. No audience had ever meant as much to me as this one.

My voice thick with emotion, my fingers shaking, and the tears in my eyes making the keys blurry, I finished the last chords of "Next to Me" from muscle memory.

"I love you, Chase," I said softly when the last note had faded.

"I love you too," he whispered back, making every wish I'd ever had come true.

I leaned over and kissed him. Not being able to get enough of him fast enough, I had my hands in his hair, on his waist, anywhere I could touch him. The kiss went from zero to one hundred in seconds, growing from sweet to filthy in a heartbeat.

I played with his full bottom lip, nipping and then soothing it with my tongue. He parted his lips for me on a moan, letting me take full control of his mouth. Holding the back of his neck, I changed my angle and went deeper. I skirted my other hand slowly up his thigh, feeling the tight fabric stretched to capacity over his hardening length, and cupped his package through his jeans, pressing just hard enough to make him groan. He pushed up into my hand, asking for more.

When I released his cock, he made a desperate sound into my mouth. I slipped my hands under his shirt, needing to feel his skin, and ran my hands over his abs. Prying my lips from his, I moved to the pulse point in his neck, kissing and sucking on it while I quickly stripped off his shirt, then mine, in rapid succession. I couldn't get over the sight of him without all of his clothes on. I didn't know if I would ever get used to how much his skin turned me on.

I dropped to my knees in front of him on the piano bench. I'd wanted to try this since he had blown my dick and my mind simultaneously that morning. I surely wouldn't be as good as he was at it, but I was making it my mission to make my guy feel amazing and sexy. If the small taste I'd had of him earlier was any indication, it would certainly be something I would enjoy too.

I rubbed my face against his still-clothed thighs, savoring the moment before it got really intense. I ran my open mouth over his heavy balls with just enough force to ensure he'd want more.

"Oh fuck!" he exclaimed as he realized what I wanted to do to him.

I licked over his bulge, savoring how aroused he was through his jeans. He threw his head back and clawed at his legs as if to stop himself from grabbing my head and forcing my mouth on him even harder.

"Carter. Baby. Please. Oh God, please," he babbled.

I took mercy on him and popped open the button on his jeans. As I lowered his zipper, I dragged my fingers along his waiting length. I slid his pants and boxer briefs over his hips in one smooth motion, only having the patience to pull them down to just below his knees. He wiggled them the rest of the way off and spread his legs eagerly.

"Probably won't be any good at this, but God, I need to taste you." I looked up at him, needy and impatient.

"If you suck cock like you kiss… gonna be great." He was panting so hard he could barely get the words out.

I chuckled and ran my tongue up the inside of his thigh as payback for his lack of help.

"Seriously, though…. Gonna be great. Focus on the head. Don't try to take it all," he advised.

His ability to string together words told me I wasn't doing my job properly. I hummed a response against his skin, moving toward my prize. I'd seen enough porn to have at least a basic understanding of how this worked, but I wanted to catch him off guard.

I started by licking one of his balls, then sucking it into my mouth, which earned me a startled cry of approval. I played with both of his balls for a minute or two, enjoying the weight of them on my tongue. Next I moved up to his cock. I licked a line with the flat of my tongue all the way up the underside to the leaking tip. I swirled my tongue over the head, matching what he had done to me this morning.

I'd had no idea the taste of him would turn me on so much. My own dick was like an iron rod in the confines of my tight jeans. I reached one hand down to adjust myself and moaned around Chase's shaft from that light pressure on my own, the vibrations from my lips pulling a reaction from him as well.

I picked up the pace, having no idea what I was doing but gauging his reactions and building on what he seemed to like. I used my hand on the base where I couldn't reach with my mouth. His pleas and whines grew louder and more urgent, the sounds going straight to my own cock. I unbuttoned the fly of my jeans one-handed, needing to relieve some of the tension, and worked us both at the same time, him with my mouth and one hand, me with the other hand. When he saw I was touching myself as well, how much I was getting off on sucking him, his eyes went dark and his erection got impossibly harder. His skin was fever hot and tight over his velvet length; tension rolled off his body as his balls drew up. He fought to keep his hips still, the need to thrust clearly overwhelming him.

"Carter... gonna make me come!"

I redoubled my efforts, sucking him forcefully. His hands slammed down on the keys behind him, making a thunderous noise at the same time as he cried out and his come pooled in my mouth. I swallowed as fast as possible, the excess dripping down my chin. The feeling of his cock tensing between my lips and the taste of his come set off my own orgasm. His cock still in my mouth, I fought the urge to bite down on him as my powerful release rocked through me.

His body went slack almost immediately after he came. I wiped the last drops of his come from my face and rested my head against his still-spread thighs, trying to catch my breath.

"Not bad for your first try. A solid six and a half," he said with a wink, patting my stubbled jaw and running his finger over my shiny bottom lip.

I caught the invading digit between my lips and gave him a teasing bite that made him squeak and pull his hand away.

"Six and a half!" I protested, pouting. "That was at least an eight. Eight and a half if you factor in my inexperience."

"Hmm." He pretended to think very carefully about it. "Maybe a six and three-quarters. A valiant effort, indeed. Bonus points for getting off on it."

I retaliated against his mocking assessment of my sexual prowess by picking him clean up off the bench, catching him off guard and causing lots of disgruntled whining. I held him carefully, wrapping his legs around me as I walked him out of the music room toward my bedroom. He was still giggling at his own wit by the time we got into the hall but sobered quickly once he saw me smiling adoringly at him. Chase had me wrapped around his little finger. There was nothing I wouldn't give him.

"I love you, C," he said, staring into my eyes.

"I love you too."

Chase

THE days and weeks flew by. We enjoyed as much time together as we could, more often spending the nights together than alone. I was busy with school as we approached the end of the year, with exams and assignments taking up the majority of my non-Carter hours.

I was happy. In a way I had never been before with any other guy or even in my life in general. Carter and I had always gotten along so well, and it seemed like we joked and laughed now as much as we had in the old days.

Plus there was the sex. My God, we were insatiable. It was like he was trying to make up for the past five years all in a few weeks. I certainly wasn't complaining. I had never been with a partner like him before; we simply could not keep our hands off each other. It was so good between us. Every time, I swore I couldn't come harder than I had the last time, and then he proved me wrong. It was like he made it his mission to find every single sensitive spot on my body and mercilessly exploit it to bring me the maximum amount of pleasure possible. We hadn't brought up anal yet. He was still so new at all this, and while I had enjoyed anal sex in the past, it wasn't a deal breaker for me if it wasn't something he was interested in. But I had to admit, with how good he was at everything else, I was curious about how amazing he would be at that too.

But there was still the looming elephant in the room we hadn't addressed—what would happen next. Inevitable Thorns were set to start recording their new album in a couple of weeks. Fortunately they had chosen a studio in Brooklyn to record at, so while Carter would be working crazy hours, we would at least get to come home to each other at the end of the day.

Carter was writing in fits and starts, whenever the inspiration struck. Thorns shared the songwriting, so the onus wasn't entirely on him, but he tended to be more of a lyricist than the other guys. He had already played around with a number of tracks over the course of their last tour, but he had yet to come up with a new song that he loved. More partially written lyrics on napkins made their way into the overflowing recycling bin each day.

I tried to stay out of his process. I didn't want to be the Yoko to the Thorns or stick my nose into their success. Their music, for the most part, was a different genre from my own, but composing was still my area of expertise. Every so often, Carter would ask for my help on a chord progression or my opinion of a tricky lyric.

Our collaboration wasn't only one-sided. I bounced ideas off him for school projects and for the few pieces I was composing on my own. I was surprised to find we were much better colleagues than we had been when we were young. We had had screaming matches growing up about writing music, and I think that's where a lot of my hesitation to get too involved came from.

More often than not, we would end up in his music room at the end of the day. We would play around together on his beautiful piano, at least until the closeness of sitting pressed together on the small bench led to our getting distracted with other things.

My friends started to suspect something was up with me. I had skipped Sunday night at Ty's for the past two weeks, giving the excuse of homework. I hadn't been texting any of my friends as frequently as I did before, and not once did I plan to meet any of them for drinks or dinner after school. I was avoiding them. It was partly because I wanted to spend as much time with Carter as possible, but also because I wasn't really sure how much to tell them. Carter and I were official with each other; we had just been too self-absorbed to bother making it a big deal publicly.

On the Sunday of the third week, Ty texted me in our group chat to check if I was coming that night, which triggered a cacophony of messages from the group trying to guilt me into it.

When Ty texted, Carter and I were in his kitchen, making sandwiches for lunch. My phone was on the counter, and after the fourth or fifth time it buzzed, Carter started teasing me about having another boyfriend. I picked up my phone, saw the chain of melodramatic messages from Ty and Graham, and rolled my eyes.

"Who is it?" Carter asked when I put my phone back on the counter without responding.

"Just some friends of mine. We always do a thing on Sunday nights, and I've blown them off the last few weeks. They're just razzing me," I said. Unfazed, I reached into the cupboard to grab us some plates.

"I didn't know that you were skipping stuff with your friends to spend time with me." Carter looked concerned. "I don't want you to feel like you can't see them because we're hanging out so much together."

"It's really not a big deal. It's not like we would be doing anything important. Plus—" I handed him his plate and kissed him lightly. "—I like spending time with you."

"Well, then, let's both go. I'd like to meet the people you hang out with." He raised an eyebrow and bit into his sandwich.

"No, it's really not a big deal, C," I said. "Let's stay in. Work on that new song we've been playing with."

I really didn't know why I had such a problem with the idea of us both going. It had nothing to do with him. I just didn't like to be the center of attention, and bringing a guy, any guy, but especially a famous one, would surely draw the focus on me.

"Please? I really don't like the thought of you ditching your friends regularly for me." Carter was clearly not going to let it go.

I relented. "Okay, if it's really that important to you. Are you sure it doesn't bother you that they know we're dating? I've kept it a little quiet because I didn't want to make a big deal out of it, or get you trailed by paparazzi or something."

"I was in the closet for a long time, babe. I'm so happy to be with you, and I never want to hide that. Let's go, please? Unless it's a no-boyfriends thing?"

I silently cursed him for being so sweet. "Fine," I conceded. "They will definitely be surprised by me bringing a boyfriend, let alone this particular boyfriend, but if you're okay with it, then I am too."

"I can't wait." He grinned at me.

Chase

WE got to Ty's a little later than we planned. Carter was so cute trying to choose what to wear to meet my friends, I couldn't help but get us distracted on the way out the door. All the usual suspects were there when we walked into Ty's.

"Well, well, well, the prodigal returns!" Ty pulled me into a hug.

"Ty, this is Carter, my... boyfriend," I said when we separated, stumbling over the unfamiliar word coming off my tongue.

C smiled at the title. It was the first time I had introduced him to someone using it, and as foreign as it felt, it sounded pretty good.

"Hey, man," Ty greeted Carter, completely cool, shaking his hand.

Ty didn't react to either the title or the fact that he clearly knew who Carter was immediately.

"'Bout time this one got a man hanging round," Ty teased me.

We stepped farther into the room. While it was busy with chatter when we arrived, it went silent when everyone noticed us. Graham was the first to speak.

"Holy shit," he said to nobody in particular.

"Um, guys, this is Carter, my boyfriend." The title came more easily the second time. I went around the room with the introductions. "C, this is Cara, Graham, Hannah, Jonathan, and his boyfriend, Jacob."

There was a chorus of hellos and various other greetings, followed by a long silence as everyone stared at us.

"So, awkward question," Graham started. Of course Graham would be the first to weigh in. "You're like... famous, right?"

Carter snorted, holding back a laugh. "I dunno, man."

"But, like, what the fuck are you doing with Boring Pants McGee over here? Does he have, like, a magic cock or something we don't know about?" Graham kept going, not picking up on Carter's sarcasm.

"Hey!" I protested, flinging the closest pillow at Graham in objection.

Carter couldn't contain himself; he laughed out loud this time at Graham's crass phrasing. He put his arms around my waist from behind, the PDA unexpected but not unwelcome. "I don't think it would be wise to answer that," Carter said over my shoulder in a solemn tone.

Then Carter brought his mouth to my ear. "I mean, he's not wrong about the magic cock part." Between his breath against my ear and the suggestion in his comment, my whole body shuddered involuntarily.

Our private exchange wasn't all that subtle, judging by the snickers that followed from around the room.

"Now, now, keep it in your boring pants, Chasey," Graham said.

"You started it, you asshole." But there was no heat behind my words.

"Seriously, though, do we get to hear the story here?" Cara asked as Carter and I settled into the love seat along one of the walls. "'Cause we all watched the *Grammys*, and it seems like our little Chasey is the guy you told the whole world you were in love with."

I rolled my eyes. Carter and I looked at each other.

"I told you we should have stayed home," I stage-whispered, making him burst out laughing again.

Even though the whole exchange was a little awkward, it also felt surprisingly comfortable. Carter seemed to be enjoying my friends—at the very least, he wasn't running away screaming from Graham. The whole thing felt... well, normal. Carter looked at me and we both shrugged, figuring we might as well tell the full story.

"Um, Chase and I met when we were young. We were best friends growing up. I guess we had feelings for each other as teenagers, but I was in denial that I was gay until a couple years ago. I did a shitty thing to him right before my family left town. It was horrible, and I've regretted it ever since. We didn't talk for a long time. I saw an opportunity to reach out to him, try to get his attention, make amends. He came to see my show a couple weeks ago, and we reconnected. Realized we both still felt there was something there, and now... things are new but really good." He slid his arm around me affectionately during the last sentence.

A chorus of "awws" followed Carter's sweet description of our relationship.

Graham broke through the moment. "I can't believe you didn't tell us! I mean, that you're fucking a rock star, obviously, but that you have some long-lost love or shit back in your life." He was mostly full of crap, but there was a little genuine hurt under the surface too.

"Yeah," Cara echoed. "We don't care who he is. We're just happy our Cinderelley finally got his felly!"

"Sorry, guys. It's only that it's so new and we're still figuring things out. I was going to say something, but I wasn't sure how to really make the whole story make sense." I grinned sheepishly. "It's a little far-fetched."

"That's okay. We're all happy for you, Chasey," Ty said, touching my hand gently.

The heat fell off Carter and me, and we slipped into regular conversation for the next couple of hours. The group was curious about Carter, but it never felt like they were grilling him for insider information or starstruck by the celebrity he had achieved. It was more that they wanted to get to know him because we were together and they were protective of my heart. They would have done the same thing for anyone who brought a new partner into the group.

The group dwindled as the night went on—people leaving to go home and get ready for the week ahead. I was half asleep on the couch, resting against Carter's strong arms. I yawned.

"Well, I think that's our cue." Carter looked at me adoringly.

"Yeah, we should take off. Thanks again, guys, for being so cool that I brought Carter with me." I shook myself, trying to wake up enough to get home.

We said our goodbyes, put on our light jackets, and headed out into the night, happy the introductions had gone so well.

Chase

"**HEY,** babe?" Carter called out to me from the sofa, where he was watching some melodramatic cooking show yet again.

We were at his place the Saturday afternoon of the week following Ty's party. Carter was gearing up to start working on Monday, rehearsing for a few days to get everything ready before they had studio time booked the following week. I was sprawled out at the kitchen table, buried chin deep in books for my final classical theory exam, which was coming up soon. It was a class that had been giving me trouble all semester, and I was ready for it to be over.

Carter and I had found our stride. I loved being around him, even if we were doing completely separate things in the same space. He had a simultaneously calming and distracting effect on me, depending on his mood and how little or how much we had been fooling around so far that day.

"Yeah?" I responded, glad to have an excuse to look up from my books for a second.

I took a sip of my cooler-than-expected tea and grimaced. *How long have I been sitting here, anyway?* I wondered to myself.

"What do you think about anal?" he asked, as if it was no bigger question than asking what I wanted for lunch today.

Tea came fountaining out of my mouth in an almost perfect comedic spit take. I quickly swiped at my notes, trying to get the drops of tea spit off before it stained the paper and rendered my writing illegible. He burst out laughing at my reaction, making me question if he was genuinely asking me my thoughts, or if he was just fucking with me.

"Uh, what?" I asked after most of the tea was cleaned up and no longer a threat to my handwritten notes.

"You heard me." He smirked. "Anal. Is that something you're interested in? Have you done it before?"

He turned off the TV and came to sit in the chair closest to me. Clearly this was going to be an actual conversation. It was something I had waited for him to bring up, but yeah, I guess it was about time we had a talk about it.

"Um, yes and yes?" I said, blushing.

"Oh yeah?"

"Are you surprised I've done it?"

"No. You're gorgeous and sexy, and any guy in his right mind would want to get as close to you as possible," he replied.

That was flattering, sure, but this conversation kept throwing me in different directions. I struggled to keep up.

I tried to pull us back to the main topic. "So are you saying it's something you want to do?"

"Is it bad if I say yes? Will you tell me what it's like?" His voice took on a softer tone now, almost wistful.

"Um, the first time's a little scary," I admitted. "There's a lot of trust involved. It's difficult to know how your body is going to react and how painful it will be."

He looked at me with concern. "Was that how it was for you?"

"For me, I didn't know the guy well enough, and I hadn't told him it was my first time, which was stupid. We rushed things more than we should have. My roommate at the time was off practicing, and we didn't know how long we had. I just wanted to get it over with, which is not the reason to have sex for the first time. It was uncomfortable, and it hurt, and I was scared to do it again for a long time."

I shrugged. The whole situation was a bad memory I didn't like to think about, but it was fair that Carter wanted to know. Carter reached for my hand, looking at me intently.

"I'm sorry it was like that for you, sweetheart," he said, the sympathy for my pain showing in his eyes.

"It was my decision. It wasn't awful—just wasn't the way I would do things again if I could. The guy and I stopped seeing each other shortly after, and it's not something I dwell on. I got what I wanted out of it at the time. The only other guy I've been with, we were seeing each other for a few weeks first. We took some more time getting me ready, and it was… good. He and I weren't a match romantically long-term, but I was grateful to him for treating me right and giving me a sense of how good sex could be."

C contemplated for a second, taking in what I'd said.

"Was it that guy you mentioned from school? Evan?" he asked. I had a feeling he got the name wrong on purpose in order to appear disinterested.

I smiled at how cute he was when he was jealous. "No, it wasn't Eli."

He relaxed a little.

"So… did you ever… top?" He hesitated as if making sure he got the terminology right. "With either of those guys?"

Shaking my head, I said, "No, never."

I assumed he was taking a moment to process the fact that I had had other partners and some less than ideal situations. His constant concern for me and regard for my happiness and feelings should at some point fail to surprise me, but he still caught me off guard every time.

"Would you want to?" he asked, his question throwing me off again.

"I don't know," I answered honestly. I had never really thought about it before, and certainly hadn't pictured doing it that way with him. It had never crossed my mind to think he would want me to top him. "Is that something you would want?"

"I think so. I mean, probably not the first time, but I want to know how it feels. And if it's something new we can do together…."

It was his turn to blush now. Carter was officially the sweetest man ever for wanting to give us a perfect first time together.

"Okay." My voice cracked with emotion. "We can do that sometime."

He smiled at me, the intensity of our conversation breaking quickly.

"But for now I want to make it not just good but *incredible* for you. Fuck the other guys who didn't know how lucky they were to be with you. I want to try to make it what you always imagined it would be."

His words broke me a little bit more. How could anyone be this wonderful? This completely perfect for me?

"You being there. That's how I always imagined it," I said simply.

Carter

THE first couple of days back with the band were long, and our progress was slow. I had been in love with the first album, and I had yet to feel that passionate about any of our new material. I had been writing a lot on the road and since we'd been back, which wasn't anything new. I wrote all the time. I was just having difficulty coming up with anything that was actually any good for the band.

What I hadn't expected was how much Chase and I had begun to write together in our spare time over the past month. I was a little apprehensive about it at the beginning; his music always tended to be more melodic, and mine had been hard rock. Our collaboration started with me asking him occasionally for his input about a note or two here and there and had grown into us full-out composing together in the evenings.

The music Chase and I created was actually really fucking good. Ideas flowed between us easily. He had a knack for taking decent lines I penned and tweaking them until they became something phenomenal. Between his formal training and my experience writing for the mass market, songs flew off the pages faster than I had ever managed on my own. I loved working with him on music. It was a connection we had always shared, and it felt so right to be doing this now.

That being said, I kept a line in the sand between the music I wrote myself and the songs that were cowritten with Chase. I didn't want to lose the identity of the Thorns or risk pissing off the band by changing up the process and overinvolving my boyfriend. The music Chase and I composed was a bit more lyrical and sophisticated than what I did with the band, but it surprised me how little it felt like a huge departure from the Thorns's first album. Nevertheless, I ultimately decided I was delusional and the music Chase and I wrote would never fit into Thorns's catalog.

So that's how it remained. My uninspired solo-written music went to the Thorns; the better songs that Chase and I had created together stayed firmly on the piano in my condo.

Frustration mounted in the rehearsal hall with each passing day. Nobody was happy with the music we were making, but none of us had an actual solution to the problem either. Beau, our keyboardist, had written one song that we all agreed would be on the record. I had two others that were good enough to be middle-track pieces, but we needed ten or so more, including a couple that would work as singles. Our studio time was coming up in a few days, and unless we developed something amazing soon, we were going to be in a very expensive pile of shit with the label.

By Thursday, we had played through every new piece any of us had written over the past year. A couple of tweaks here and there and we still only had four, maybe five, songs that we all agreed on. We were stressed and agitated, the pressure of our anticipated sophomore album looming. This was the make-or-break album for many bands; we were trying to get past the one-hit-wonder category, and we were terrified of being a promising band turned has-beens in the blink of an eye.

I realized more and more that the timeline they had given us was insane. We barely had the opportunity to rest and recuperate from the tour before we were expected to start all over again with new material we had somehow come up with in our spare time. We needed a break. We needed to reconnect on a personal level and fuel the chemistry between us that made the first album work so well.

By six o'clock we were all fried. Exhausted and emotionally burned out from working so much for such little reward. I invited the guys over to my place to grab some food and chill in the hope of taking some of the stress off. We would all have to go hard for the next few days.

All three of my bandmates, Beau, Dean, and Asher, agreed to come home with me. We got there about an hour later with pizza, beer, and a new racing game to load up on the Xbox. We all relaxed into the game, enjoying the food and drinks, and equally enjoying shit-talking each other's lack of driving skills. It was a good idea, and some of the constant stress of the past week began to lessen.

Dean and Beau were super competitive with each other and won the majority of the races. I held my own, but Ash was terrible and got his ass kicked nearly every game.

"What's wrong with you? How are you so bad at this?" Dean started yelling at Ash after one particularly bad round.

Ash was equally worked up about the stupid game. "Fuck you! The buttons keep fucking me up. I forget which one does what. This game is too fucking complicated. Just give me a joystick and let me drive!"

"You play the drums. Aren't there, like, a million of them too? How can you remember which drum to hit but you can't remember the A button is for Accelerate?" Dean threw his hands up in the air in exasperation.

Beau and I were dying laughing at their exchange. It felt so good to be back with the guys, focusing on something that wasn't music or our failure in the rehearsal hall this week. We needed to do this more. We'd practiced, played, and relied on each other for so many years while we tried to break into music. We'd lived together on the bus for so many months on tour. Somewhere along in the process, we'd forgotten how to be friends.

I had gotten up to grab a couple more beers from the fridge when there was a knock at the door. I didn't think any of the management team I had invited were going to be able to make it, but if they had decided to come late, the more the merrier. I opened the door to find my beautiful boyfriend standing in front of me.

We hadn't spent much time together over the past week because of my rehearsal schedule and his upcoming exams. We had been texting, but even that wasn't consistent, and I missed being with him regularly. I broke into a grin when I saw him standing there, excited he felt secure enough in our relationship to stop by unannounced and looking forward to finally introducing him to my bandmates.

"Hey, sweetheart." I leaned in to kiss him. "What are you doing here?"

"Hi, C. I think I may have left a book here last weekend. Have you seen it around?"

"Umm, I don't think so. What does it look like?"

"It's a big textbook. Blue with some big uglyass photo on the front of a conductor and orchestra. It's for my twentieth century music history class."

"I haven't seen it, but let me help you look."

Chase walked a little farther into the foyer and noticed the guys still yelling at each other over the stupid game.

"Oh shit. I didn't realize you had people over. I can come back," Chase said, turning toward the door.

"Nah," I said, trying to sideline his fear about barging in. "It's just the guys from the band. We had another rough day today, so we needed a little decompression. Stay. I'll introduce you to them, we'll find your book, and then you can hang out. I want them to get to know you."

"I dunno...."

"Please? Have you eaten? There's lots of pizza. I've talked about you nonstop. They probably think you're my imaginary boyfriend who's way too good for me."

I couldn't seem to stop blathering. Now that he was here, I realized how much I'd missed having him with me this week and was determined to convince him to stick around for a little while at least.

"Fine," he agreed. "Book first, then pizza."

"Hey, guys!" I said loudly to pull their attention away from whatever they were currently arguing about.

The room finally went silent. Ash took the opportunity to pry his controller back out of Dean's hands after Dean had apparently decided Ash wasn't good enough to deserve it.

"Guys, this is my boyfriend, Chase. Chase, that's Dean, Beau, and Asher. Ignore them fighting like children." I was proud to introduce all the most important people in my life to each other.

"Damn, man. You didn't tell us how cute he was. What the fuck is he doing with your sorry ass?" Dean asked, shaking Chase's hand.

Chase blushed bright red and giggled nervously. Dean was absolutely straight and was the opposite of me in the "falling into bed with willing groupies" category. But we loved him just the same. He was well intentioned, if a little slutty.

"Chase is a composition student at Julliard," I boasted. "He came by to look for a book he left here."

"He brags about you constantly," Ash confided to Chase with a wink. "You've got him under some fierce spell."

After a few more minutes of ribbing, Chase and I excused ourselves to look for his textbook.

"Suuuuure. Looking for a 'textbook,'" Dean said, throwing in air quotes for comedic effect. "Where's the book, Cart? Buried in his a—"

"Okay!" I cut him off loudly.

I really did not want to go down that road with Dean, especially since Chase and I still hadn't actually done that. Dean and the other guys were laughing hysterically at finally having the opportunity to razz me about my previously nonexistent sex life.

"Back in a minute!" I called over my shoulder as Chase and I hightailed it out of the room.

Chase

CARTER and I looked everywhere, but we couldn't find my textbook, which was a really big deal because I had an exam in that class on Monday, and the stupid thing had cost me over a hundred bucks and had a bunch of my notes in it.

"Still no luck?" Beau called to us from down the hall.

"No, can't find it anywhere!" I called back.

"Okay, boys. It's time to step in," Dean said.

They all got up from their seats in the living room and came into the music room to help us search.

"What's this?" Beau asked after a minute or two of hunting with no success.

He was standing next to the piano, looking at the music to one of the songs Carter and I had been fooling around with last weekend. I had completely forgotten that it was there and hadn't thought to tuck it away before the band came barging in.

I didn't know how Carter felt about sharing what we had written with the guys. I had assumed it would be too soft to be something he thought the band would be interested in. Most of the Thorns were of the rock/heavy rock persuasion. While Carter and I had combined our styles for the music we had been toying with, it was definitely not as hard core as the music the band usually played. Well, with the exception of "Next to Me," the one ballad Carter wrote for me.

"Oh, um, nothing." I tried to grab the sheets out of Beau's hand before he could look too closely, not wanting to embarrass Carter with the band finding out we were writing something they might make fun of.

"No, it's not." Beau kept the sheet music away from me.

Why am I always the shortest one in the room? I thought to myself. I didn't know much about Beau, but from the way Carter talked about him, I got the impression they were closer than Carter was with the other guys in the band.

Beau looked at the written music intently and then switched his gaze between me and Carter. Carter and I made eye contact across the room while Beau was looking at the pages. I threw him a panicked look, silently willing him to let me know what he wanted me to do. Carter shrugged, seemingly unbothered by the situation.

"Cart, what is this?" Beau repeated after studying the rest of the pages for a bit. If he read music like I did, he was hearing the notes on the page clearly in his mind. "Have we seen this one already?"

"No," Carter answered nonchalantly. "Chase and I have been collaborating a little in our spare time. Playing with some melodies and shit for fun."

"Guys, this is really good. Why haven't you shown us?" Beau sat on the piano bench and put the music back on the stand in front of him.

He started to play the song Carter and I had written. This piece was still in progress. A couple of others we had been working on were closer to being done, but C and I were both happy with how this piece was coming together. We had titled it simply, "Lost." The lyrics were about being turned around in the woods and struggling to find the way out, a metaphor for the mental struggle of finding oneself.

Beau's style of playing was very different from mine. I wasn't a concert pianist like a lot of my colleagues at Julliard by any stretch of the imagination, but I was classically trained and could hold my own in a formal setting. Beau was a professional musician in a completely different genre than the people I was used to being around. His fingering was a little clunky, and his carriage movements were stiff, but the passion behind each note was invigorating. It was like he was making a point of not following the rules, focusing on the music instead of the technique. There was something incredibly exhilarating about that.

I was mesmerized listening to Beau play our song. The other guys clearly felt the same way. Everyone slowly drifted closer to the piano, and we were all in a small circle with Beau in the center by the time the last notes rang out.

Ash broke the silence when Beau finished playing. "Holy shit! Are there lyrics?"

"Yeah," Beau said before Carter or I could respond.

He read the words like a poem. His phrasing was different from how it would have been if he sang it, but he got the point across nonetheless.

"Fuck, guys. That's better than any of the bullshit we've been working on this week. And you wrote it just like that?" Dean asked.

I hesitated. "Well, this one's not done yet. We're still working on it."

"There are more?" Dean exclaimed.

C and I nodded in unison.

"Why the hell haven't we been playing this?" Dean asked again.

Beau reached out from his seat and touched my arm gently. I was getting a gay—or at least bi—vibe from him but had no idea what his deal was. He was cute in kind of a boy-next-door-turned-rocker way but in no way compared to the beauty of my actual boy-next-door-turned-rocker.

"Chase, this is amazing. You're a composer?" Beau asked.

"Yeah. Well, I want to be." I decided to go with the full explanation once I got a sense Carter wouldn't be upset with me for saying something. "We wrote this together, though. It wasn't only me." I looked at Carter with affection. "It's just… not the usual type of stuff you guys do. I didn't want to overstep or assume my stuff would be anywhere near good enough for you."

"You're right. It's better than what we do," Beau said. "It's not as hard, but Ash can throw in a crazy beat. Maybe speed it up a little?"

Ash nodded enthusiastically. Beau looked through the music again to find the chorus. His fingers brushed the keys, and he started to play, faster than before.

As an adult, I had never been overly possessive about the music I wrote. I had appreciated getting constructive critiques from mentors and other collaborators. I think that's why Carter and I were working so well together these days. We wrote like a team. No ego, no objections to well-intended feedback, just the focus on making the music the best it could be.

Beau played with the song over and over, making slight changes each time until he found a tempo he was happy with. I actually liked it more that way than as the slow ballad it was when we began. It was less predictable, more original, like something I had never heard before.

Carter grabbed his old acoustic guitar off the wall. We had only written the piano chords, but he started to jam along with Beau, making up the guitar part on the spot and singing the lyrics we wrote from memory.

C didn't have a full drum set at home, but he had a couple of handheld drums and other percussion instruments. They were more for show than for use, but Ash pulled one of the djembe's off the top shelf and sat down on the floor next to the piano. He tested the sound of the djembe with his open palms, looking satisfied with the variety of tones he could produce on the small drum. The beat was rough without a full kit, but it added to the pace of the song and gave an idea of what it would sound like.

Finally, Dean sourced out the one bass guitar in Carter's collection. He got a feel for the weight of the unfamiliar instrument and found a small amp to plug it into. He spent a few minutes tuning, as it had been sitting unused for a long time. Then Dean joined in with the other three, adding the lower register and bringing the song to life with a steady heartbeat.

The whole makeshift session came together quickly. It was inspiring to see them fooling around on somewhat foreign gear but still replicating what they wanted to do when they got their regular instruments back in their hands. They read each other well. When one moved to solo or do something fancy, the others would back off a little quite naturally.

The song started to meld into shape—a guitar solo came together for Carter, and backup vocals were first tentative and then became more sure, adding depth to the lyrics. I was standing next to them all in awe, listening to the music swirl around me.

While I had fancied myself an amateur composer for a lot of years, I was completely out of my depth. Despite the fact that I was dating the lead singer, the band was made up of Grammy Award winning professionals. I was just a student with a big dream, and I had no idea if it would ever amount to a career.

The music was like nothing I had ever worked on before. They made it their own, yet it stayed remarkably true to what Carter and I had written. The goose bumps and the happy tears were right below the surface while the guys got more and more into the song. My music, our music, was coming to life before my eyes on a professional scale. I was inspired and grateful, proud and motivated to keep working.

After about half an hour of playing around with the song, it reached a point of consistency. The cracks had settled, and a couple of the sections Carter and I were still having difficulty with had ironed themselves into a shape that both we and the rest of the band were happy with. Carter walked to the kitchen to grab some water for everyone.

"Chase, that's a seriously cool song," Dean said. "You guys are crazy talented together. You never wanted to write rock music? You could totally do it, you know. A ton of bands would kill for shit like this."

"Absolutely," Ash chimed in. "You could sell it super easily."

"So, guys, are we all agreed this goes on the album? This is our single, right?" Beau asked the band when Carter came back into the music room.

"Absol-fuckin'-lutely,"   Dean   responded emphatically.

"It's Chase and Carter's song. They haven't even said if we can use it yet," Ash said. "But if they're cool and it sounds as good as I think it will with the full kit, I'm down with it being the single."

Carter looked at me, questioning if I was okay with this. I nodded subtly at him, trying to convey my enthusiasm and telling him everything he needed to know with my eyes alone.

"If you guys like it and Chase is in, I'm on board," Carter agreed.

"Chase?" Beau looked up at me.

"Of course I'm in. It sounds unreal, guys," I said, trying to not blubber and yet wanting to emphasize how completely into them using the song I was.

"Then it's settled," Beau proclaimed. "We have a single. Now… show us the rest of them!"

Chase

THE guys spent the next several hours going through every song Carter and I had written in much the same way as they'd done with "Lost." There were one or two that they decided didn't fit, but for the most part, they loved what we had done, and with some minor tweaks, the songs sounded like the Thorns.

They played through the night, stopping only a few times for snacks and short breaks. When the temperature dropped, Dean reached for his jacket, which was draped over an end table, inadvertently revealing my long-forgotten misplaced textbook. He apologized over and over, but I paid him no mind. Without that mishap—a simple chance encounter that delayed me from finding my book—one of the greatest evenings of my life would have never taken place. Sending up a silent thank-you to fate, I got my ass back to work.

I pulled up a chair next to the piano Beau had commandeered, and as much as they wanted to keep their identity, they surprised me by how much input they asked me for. It wasn't ever like they were taking my work away from me. It was a team effort, and I was as much a part of it as any of the bandmates.

Somewhere around 4:00 a.m., we all started to get a little hazy, and Ash decided we should call it a night. The progress over the course of the evening had been insane, and they were all stoked to try it out with their full gear and show it to the higher-ups the next day. The guys finally left Carter and me alone in his condo, and he wrapped his arms around me as soon as he had locked the front door.

"I am so proud of you, Chase. You were amazing tonight. Are you sure this is okay? It's your work, and I don't want you to feel pressured to let the band use it."

"It's *our* work," I stressed. "And you and I may have started writing it, but you guys made the songs come alive. They sound like Inevitable Thorns *and* like us, and I couldn't be happier about this. This was an amazing night." I kissed him softly.

"They loved you," he said with a yawn as we quickly got ready for bed.

"That's good, because I love *you*."

"I love you too, baby. So much." He turned off the bedside lamp and snuggled me close, spooning me from behind. I didn't think I had ever been so happy.

Carter

I WOKE up the next morning when Chase said goodbye before he left for class. We hadn't gotten more than a couple hours sleep, and while I didn't have to be at the rehearsal hall for a while yet, Chase had an early start on Fridays at school. I felt bad for keeping him up so late the night before, knowing he was stressed about his studies and was in the middle of exams. He'd sworn he didn't mind and wanted to stay with us the handful of times I'd asked him if he needed to go to bed, but I felt guilty for it nonetheless. I went back to sleep for another hour, drifting off as soon as he left.

My alarm woke me with a start. I rolled my ass out of bed and into the shower. The hot water worked some magic on my tired muscles and woke me up a little. I scrubbed down quickly as I had set my alarm for as late as possible and needed to move fast to get to the rehearsal hall in Brooklyn on time. I threw on some comfortable clothes, caring more about what I sounded like than what I looked like. I guzzled one cup of coffee quickly and grabbed a second cup for the road, along with a banana. I made it to the hall with ten minutes to spare. Early was on time in our line of work, and pulling the diva card due to lack of sleep didn't fly in my books.

Beau was already there, sipping his coffee on the couch in the lounge area. He looked surprisingly awake for how little rest we'd all gotten. A minute after I arrived, Ash and Dean came in together with a massive box of pastries for everyone. I grabbed a chocolate donut, starting to feel a little more human with the caffeine and sugar in my system.

The four of us all zonked out on the sofa while we waited to be told what to do. We were awake and functioning but saving our energy for the rehearsal.

"All right!" Cory said loudly to grab everyone's attention. "What did you guys want to start with today? The song we left off on yesterday?"

"Actually," Beau started, speaking for the group, "we had some inspiration last night and have some new stuff we want to try."

The rest of us voiced our agreement.

"Good. What you had was crap. Hope you got your heads out of your asses and this sucks less." Delicacy was not in Core's repertoire.

We moved into the rehearsal space itself and took our familiar positions at our stands. I picked up my guitar, my fingers a little tender from overuse on the strings last night, but nothing I hadn't dealt with before. Beau called out the name of the song, "Lost," the first one we'd practiced last night and decided would be the single.

"This may be a little rough to begin with. We need to figure out the drum lines still, but it's a start," he called to Cory, who nodded at us.

We played through the song once and then stopped so Ash could work through a couple of things on his own. Even last night, with the makeshift setup, it had sounded like something special after we'd fiddled with it. Today, with the full gear, even with some tinkering left to do, it was outstanding. I was as in love with this piece as I was with the songs on the first album (with the exception of Chase's song, which would forever be in its own category). We were on fire again, for the first time in what felt like ages.

The atmosphere in the hall was noticeably less tense than it had been the past few days. We were joking around a little more, and the satisfaction that we actually had something we were all happy with showed in all of us. We played through the song again, getting the full feel of the drums, the beat coming through like a train and the high hats and cymbals making this the rock piece it truly was.

Cory stopped us at the end. "Holy fuck, guys. Where the hell did that come from?"

"Carter and his boyfriend, Chase, wrote it," Ash said. "We changed it up a little. But good, yeah?"

"Hell yes, it's good. Better than good," Cory agreed. "That's the single?"

"Yeah, we think so." I nodded. "There are some others we want to include on the album too, but that's the single."

We went through the song a few more times, playing with a few last things we wanted to try before it was perfect. After about an hour or so on the same song, we took a five-minute break. I grabbed the opportunity to text Chase, letting him know Cory was happy with the song and was going to send the cell phone video recording he took to the label for final approval. He was sure they would be as crazy about it as we all were.

Chase's response was immediate and was just a string of emojis. Some had huge smiling faces, some had stars for eyes, one or two were even crying happy tears. Getting to share this with my guy made the process feel even sweeter.

After our short break, we got back to work and played through the rest of the songs we had agreed to on the previous night. Cory seemed as happy with the rest of the tunes as he was with the first one. He took short video clips of the chorus of each song after we had finished working it. My voice was getting a little rough after a couple of hours, and we took a break with sandwiches we'd had delivered.

About halfway through lunch, Chase texted me to say he was outside and asked if someone could let him in. I headed around back to open the door for him and pulled him into the dim hallway. He had gone back to his place to freshen up and change after class, and damn, did he look good.

He had on these tight heather-gray jeans that made his ass look downright edible. He was wearing a pale blue polo and a lightweight cobalt-colored hoodie. His blond hair was styled the way he normally did it, with just enough product to make it stay where he wanted but still look sexy and disheveled. He had an olive-green canvas messenger bag slung across his chest, probably filled with schoolbooks in case there was any downtime for him to get some studying done. His face had a slight flush to it, as though he had been walking quickly from the subway in order to get here faster.

I pulled him against me in the hall, unable to resist cupping his perfect ass with both my hands. I kissed him firmly, leaving him gasping at my sudden assault. God, I had missed him so much. His mind, his body. Talking with him. Kissing him. It had only been a couple of days since we'd spent time together alone—at least when we were awake—but I was already going crazy needing to be with him.

"Fuck, you look good," I said before I licked into his mouth.

His response was to kiss me with more intensity, pressing me against the cold wall and rutting into me until we were both hard and panting.

"Don't wanna stop, but we should get up there before they figure out what we're doing," I managed to get out between kisses.

"Mmf," he protested against my lips, making it more difficult each second to pull away.

He drew himself back. "Tonight?" he bartered.

"Oh fuck yes," I agreed quickly.

We walked slowly to the rehearsal hall, giving our bodies a chance to calm down before we had to be decent in front of the others. It was going to be a long afternoon.

Chase

"CHASE the boyfriend!" Dean greeted me with a handshake and a bro hug that I was absolutely not cool enough to pull off.

"Dean the bass!" I responded, mirroring his greeting.

"Dude, this guy is the reason why you're not tearing us a new one today," Dean said to Cory, pointing down at me over my head.

"Nice to see you again, man," Cory said with a wave, his mouth full of sandwich. "Hear things worked out pretty good with this one." He gestured to Carter, raising his eyebrows suggestively.

"Yeah, guess they did." I blushed at Carter.

"Also, these assholes have more than four shitty chords to give me today. So thanks for that. You're a songwriter?" Cory continued.

Dean, my new biggest fan, bragged on my behalf. "Not just a writer, a composer. Julliard."

"I'm only a student right now, but hopefully someday," I said, not wanting to oversell myself.

"Impressive. Well this shit's gonna be huge, so you'll be a lot more than 'only a student' when it gets out you cowrote Inevitable Thorns's next Grammy-winning song. Good job, kid." Cory finished off his sandwich and licked his fingers sloppily. "All right, you lazy freeloaders, back to work!"

The guys went back to their places, throwing away their trash on the way.

"Next Grammy-winning song!" Carter echoed Cory's words in my ear gleefully before leaning down to kiss me quickly on the cheek.

He headed to his mic stand, grinning at me while I tried to process Cory's praise.

Holy shit, what if that happened? I had gone from being a mediocre student—at an admittedly fancy school—to a promising rock-music composer with songs about to be on an album of a well-known band, in the space of less than twenty-four hours. Aspiration and potential swirled in the pit of my stomach. I had been passionate about what I did for forever, but it had always seemed so far away. Keep taking lessons. Get into a good school. Get decent grades and make important connections. Graduate. Spend a bunch of years interning while living in poverty, kissing ass, and keeping my fingers crossed for an eventual lucky circumstance that might lead to a possibly successful break.

It felt like I had inadvertently skipped over a bunch of the bullshit, temporarily at least. I didn't want to count my chickens, but this was a huge opportunity for me. To think that it came from writing music with

Carter the way we had tried to do since we were in elementary school made it even more unreal.

Ash counted the band in with his drumsticks, muting my train of thought. I listened to one of the songs they had been working on last night, and fuck, Cory was right, they did sound fantastic. It was even better with the full drum kit; the song came alive with Ash's pulsing beat. I relaxed into the couch, listening in awe for hours and watching my man sing the shit out of the lead vocals we wrote together.

Chase

"YOU know what I'm thinking?" Carter asked as we made our way from the subway down the block to my place later that evening. The sun was starting to dip below the horizon. It was a beautiful sunset. All the oranges and pinks set fire to the sky. The clouds were fluffy and delicate. The air had warmed a little, and it was turning into a lovely spring. We held hands as we walked down the street, both high off a good day in the rehearsal hall.

"What?" I asked, a smile in my voice. I brought our joined hands to my lips to kiss his fingers.

"Breakfast for dinner. How does that sound?"

"Oh my God," I groaned, my stomach rumbling at the thought of food. "So good. I think I even have some bacon. Fuck, that sounds amazing."

"Well, if I had known the suggestion would have made you basically come all over yourself…," he teased into my ear, chuckling at my reaction.

I reached over and hit his chest playfully with the back of my open hand.

We got to my apartment. I let us inside and tossed the keys into the bowl next to the door. Carter had only been here a few times. We tended to go to his place because it was more convenient when I was coming from school, and well, it was nicer. I liked my place, but there was a big difference between the kind of an apartment and amenities a student could afford versus a successful musician. I was proud of the fact that I lived by myself. I'd had roommates up until this year, but I had worked my ass off last year applying for and receiving quite a few small scholarships, as well as teaching music lessons in my spare time, in order to afford the extravagance of living alone.

"Actually—" Carter picked up our earlier conversation, gripping the front of my shirt and kissing my neck at the collar where I had left the buttons open. "—I changed my mind. There's another way I would rather make you come than with breakfast food."

I shuddered at his sexy innuendo. He began slowly planting openmouthed kisses in a straight line up my throat and over my chin. His lips were lush and plump. Each kiss left enough moisture on my neck to make me shiver at the loss of contact when he moved on. He smelled incredible, like the pine aftershave I had grown to associate with him. It made me hard instantly now—like a Pavlovian response.

Before I started seeing Carter, going for months without any sort of sexual contact with another person didn't bother me too much, but after a few weeks of getting off with him almost daily, a couple of days of abstinence had made me horny as fuck.

Carter knew how much he was turning me on. He was just as hard as I was, our clothed groins lining up and providing a sweet pressure. He shifted slightly to put his thigh in between my legs, giving me something to press against and making my jeans even tighter.

"God, you were driving me crazy today," he said. "Watching me. Wearing those fucking sexy-as-fuck pants. Please tell me you're ready. I need to be inside you tonight."

He attacked my neck again, off to the side this time. I was sure he was going to leave a mark, considering how deeply he was sucking and biting me, but I couldn't bring myself to care even a little. Let him mark me. I was his either way.

"Oh fuck. Yes. Carter. Please." I tilted my neck for him to abuse further.

His hands on my hips guided me into the bedroom. His lips never left my neck. He was working that impossibly good spot behind my ear that turned me on like nobody's business when our legs finally hit my bed.

We scrambled to undress each other, our limbs flailing as the need to get skin to skin overwhelmed us. When we were finally naked, I was close to unraveling. His skin was hot to the touch, almost feverish. His hands were glued to my ass, kneading and stroking the muscles. He kept moaning my name like a mantra. His cock was flush with mine, rocking against me over and over. At this rate, I had no idea how he would ever get inside me before we both came. I was so turned on that coming from no more than this was a real possibility. But I didn't want that. I needed to finally know what fucking felt like with him.

Since my last boyfriend made me realize how much I actually loved having something up there, I had been getting off regularly with a couple of toys I'd bought, but it had been so long since I'd had an actual dick inside me, my ass was already clenching with eagerness.

Carter caressed my body, touching every part of me that was sensitive to him, awakening all my nerve endings. He sucked on my nipples, making me pant and my cock leak. His hands found my abs, and he drew little circles over them with his fingertips. He kissed the inside of my wrist, right on my pulse point. When I finally couldn't wait any longer, I reached over to my bedside table to grab the lube and a condom; the latter I had fortunately had the foresight to buy a week or two ago. When he saw the supplies, I felt his heart rate shoot up, and then he attacked my mouth with vigor and intent.

"God, C, please!"

I was getting close to shooting already, and I needed him to pick up the pace if we didn't want this to be over before it began. His body was tense, his hands trembling slightly.

He wet his fingers with lube and brought them slowly behind my ballsac. His eyes locked with mine as he lowered his fingers, millimeter by millimeter. When he brushed my hole for the first time, fireworks shot behind my eyes. My skin became oversensitive, and I thought for a terrible second I was going to come right then. I thankfully managed to get myself under control and hold it off. I inhaled deeply, and his chest rumbled above me to match the humor in his eyes, despite the intensity of the moment.

"That sensitive?" he asked with reverence.

I nodded, biting my bottom lip. "So good," I moaned.

His fingers circled my ring for a minute or two, teasing the hell out of me and reducing me to noises instead of words. His eyes never left mine, like he was in a daze from watching how turned on I was. His middle finger finally pushed in slightly, breaching my entrance. I did this enough to myself that it didn't feel foreign or uncomfortable, even at the beginning. It was just a mind trip that it was him finally touching that part of me.

I'd lost track of the number of times I had gotten off to the thought of having sex with him, both when we were in high school and since we had reconnected. He was my go-to fantasy, and I was about to learn if the reality measured up to my many vivid imaginings.

His agile finger worked its way deeper, relaxing my muscles and getting me ready for him. I was about to complain that he needed to move faster when the first finger slid all the way out and was joined with a second. My body sucked in the two digits easily. He groaned, watching his fingers disappear inside me.

"Fuck, Chase. You're so fucking hot, baby. You're doing so good. So damn sexy." His babble soothed me.

He worked the two fingers inside me farther, fucking me with them faster and faster. He opened them wide to stretch me. My cock was throbbing with want against my stomach. I didn't dare touch it, or I would absolutely come instantly.

"C, I'm ready, please. You need to fuck me. Please," I begged him, not caring how needy I sounded.

He pulled his fingers from my body. I almost wept at the loss of the pressure. He grabbed the condom from the table and struggled with it for a second. I took it from him and quickly opened it, slid it over his thick waiting length, and added some more lube.

"Gaahh!" He exhaled when I touched his unbearably hard erection. "Don't touch me too much or I'll come. Need to be in you."

"Yes, now. Please, C," I whimpered.

I lay on my back, opened my knees, and he slid in between my legs. He guided his cock to my waiting hole, holding it there and taking a shaky breath as if to steady himself. The pressure of his dick against me was driving me insane. I needed him to move. He pushed slightly, tentatively. I reached around and grabbed his ass, encouraging him to push harder and keep going. His cock slid through the first ring of muscles, the head popping in easily.

"Oh fuck!" he cried out. "You're so tight. Fuck!"

"More. Keep going, please. I need more."

He slid inside me, inch by glorious inch. The pressure was amazingly intense. He was so thick I felt stretched more than I ever had been. I wanted to weep at the fullness when he was finally completely seated. God, he felt so perfect. The need to move was overwhelming. From the sounds he was making already, I knew he wouldn't last long either, but Christ, I needed him to fuck me before we both lost it. He pulled out a little and made a couple of shallow strokes, testing what felt good for both of us.

His confidence grew quickly. His thrusts became more forceful and deeper; he pulled almost all the way out before plunging back inside me hard and fast. He changed the angle slightly, skimming my prostate with the head of his cock. I shouted with that move, begging him to keep hitting me there.

"Oh God, Chase, you feel so good. Baby, oh fuck. I'm so close," he moaned.

He took me more forcefully with each pass, nailing my gland with way more accuracy than he should have been capable of his first time. He reached for my aching erection, and as soon as he stroked me once, I immediately came over his hand, crying his name on each pulse. He thrust twice more, and then he was there too, pounding his release into my waiting body. His orgasm seemed to last forever, and he was a shaking mess once it finally subsided. He pulled out gently and got rid of the condom before collapsing alongside me, his breathing still sounding fast and unsteady.

"That was…," he started, then trailed off, his eyes unfocused but his smile wide.

"That was fucking amazing," I finished for him.

Chase

THE band worked through the weekend, refining the songs and getting them ready to record the following week. I spent the weekend on the couch in the rehearsal hall with them, my study materials surrounding me and my focus divided between the music the Thorns were playing and the music my books taught me about. The live version was unquestionably more interesting, but as difficult as it was to concentrate, I forced myself to prepare for my last exams coming up in the following days.

Carter was bouncing off the walls on Sunday evening, awash with the need to get started laying down the tracks. He was so enthusiastic about the new catalog the Thorns had been working on the past few days it was hard to not find his excitement contagious.

Monday morning went by so slowly I thought it would never end. It was the final lecture of the semester, so it was basically a review session with no new material. I found it nearly impossible to pay attention to what was going on and not let my mind wander to the recording studio in Brooklyn.

I had the exam for the music history class in the afternoon, and at two o'clock, when it was over, I was out the door like a shot. I made my way through the subway and over to Brooklyn as fast as the transit system let me, tapping my fingers anxiously on my messenger bag the whole trip, my stomach in knots, hoping the label would like what they heard.

When I reached the studio, the band was in the middle of a song behind the glass. The studio technicians were working to capture what Thorns was performing, and Cory sat on the edge of his chair, nervously chewing a pencil. I came in quietly and found a stool as out of the way as possible. They played for another few minutes, finishing the song on a flourish. Cory flipped a button and talked to the band for a second through the microphone.

"That's great, guys. Let's do it one more time. Cart, you can go a little harder on the vocal runs after the second chorus. Play with it. Don't hold back. Guys, let him go where he needs to with that part. If he goes longer, stay with him. See what happens with that." Cory turned to me after he was done addressing the band. "Hey, man."

"Hey. How are they doing so far?" I asked.

"It's going really well. We're almost done with this first track, and then we'll see if we can bang one more out today, depending on how Carter's feeling. Don't want to blow out his voice on the first day."

"Good stuff," I responded absently, waving to C when he noticed I was there.

"Gonna be a fucking good album," one of the technicians chimed in. "It'll be a hit. The label will probably want it done quickly so they can be touring by the end of the summer."

My stomach dropped at his words.

"Yeah, hoping to go international this time," Cory mumbled, his focus on the band as they got ready to go again. "It's gonna be huge."

I tensed on my stool. Waves of panic hit me quickly. My heart started hammering, though my blood ran cold. Their words rang in my brain. International tour. Leaving in the summer. I had been focusing so much on their new songs, I hadn't processed the timeline. Of course the label would want them to tour right away.

Ash counted the band in, and they started the song again, but the noise was muffled in my ears. Things between Carter and me were so damn good right now; how was I going to be okay with him up and leaving for who knows how long?

I struggled to take a deep breath, a full-out anxiety attack coming on. I needed to get out of that room. I needed to get some air.

Although I tried to leave quickly without being noticed, I fumbled around getting up and struggled to find the handle to the door with my shaking hands. Cory glanced back at me, then quickly returned his attention to the band. Tears stung my eyes. I stumbled through the door and walked hastily and unevenly back through the halls I had been so keyed up to traverse such a short time before.

I shoved through the door to the exit, wheezing as I made it outside. The bright sunlight made me squint and struggle to see properly. I backed up against the cool exterior brick wall, doubling over with my hands on my knees, gasping for air. International tour. End of the summer.

I fought for control, but the first heavy tears started to fall almost immediately. Time got away from me, but at least ten minutes must have passed before the door beside me opened. Carter's arms were around me before I processed that he was standing there, his presence causing me to break down even more.

"Sweetheart! What happened?" he asked.

"I... I...."

I was trembling and couldn't come up with words, so I just let him hold me. He rubbed my back and whispered soothing words into my ear. It seemed to take forever, but eventually I calmed down enough to respond.

"Chase. Baby. You gotta tell me what's wrong." Carter's eyes were full of concern.

"It's stupid." I sniffed. "They were talking about you going back on tour soon, a big international tour, and I freaked out a little. But it's fine. I know it's part of your job. I knew this would happen." I tried to downplay my emotions, but I don't think he bought it.

C held me tighter for a moment, then pulled back to wipe my tears with his fingers and kiss their tracks on my cheeks.

"Nothing has been decided yet," he said. "Hell, this is the first time I'm hearing of it, so it's just speculation." He paused, then proceeded cautiously. "Honestly, they're probably right, though. The album is going to be amazing. Thanks to you." His words were meant to reassure me, to help calm me down. "We all knew a tour would come eventually. If not this summer, by the fall for sure."

I attempted a joke through my tears, uncomfortable with the intensity. "Should have let you use those shitty songs you guys started with."

He laughed halfheartedly. "Never. This is *our* album. You and me and the band. I've never been prouder of any work I've done in my life." He paused again, not letting my weak effort at humor distract him. "Talk to me, Chase case. Is it just the possibility of me leaving?"

I sighed, trying to make sense of my messed-up emotions, not wanting to seem like a ridiculous teenager. "I guess… the last time you left… it was so long. I'm scared these past few months have been too good to be true. What if you leave for good again?" I asked, voicing the doubt in the back of my mind.

"I won't," he said. "Before, I was scared and not ready to be honest with you. With myself. I've been in love with you for ten years, Chase. You're my heart, babe. I don't want to go any more than you want me to. But I will come back. I just want to make sure that's enough. I want to make sure that touring isn't a deal breaker, because I can promise to come back, but I'm not sure I can promise not to go. I wish I could say that I didn't have to, but it's up to the label, and if I don't go, the band can't go."

The door flew open, breaking the moment.

"Cart, need you back. Break's over." Cory's voice through the half-open door was clipped, and he left before Carter acknowledged his instructions.

Carter stroked my face softly. "Come back inside? Please? I really want you to see how good our songs are. But I want to keep talking about this later."

I nodded. I still felt like a horse had kicked me in the stomach, but I took a deep breath and followed him back into the studio for the rest of the session.

Carter

THE remainder of the week passed uneventfully, if a little awkwardly. Inevitable Thorns was making progress every day in the studio, churning out amazing tracks and sounding better on each number. I was worried about Chase more each day. He seemed to be back to himself after his anxiety attack at the session on Monday. He was there with us whenever he didn't have an exam, and his presence motivated me even more to make this album the best it could be. But something was still off.

Chase and I spent the evenings hanging out, watching stupid movies or playing video games, joking and fucking like nothing had shifted. But I would occasionally catch him lost in thought in a private moment or looking at me when he thought I wouldn't notice. His gaze was a million miles away, filled with a heaviness that hadn't been there before.

I didn't know what to do. I knew something was wrong and we needed to return to the conversation we'd had outside the studio, but I didn't know what to say to not make things worse. So I avoided the situation and focused on being the best boyfriend to him I could be in every other way.

After three weeks in the studio, the album was fully recorded. The band was ecstatic about the final product, happy our work was done, and glad to be passing along the torch to the audio engineers to make us sound even better.

It would take a month or two of postproduction to get the album ready to be released. The label seemed to be in full support of our new material and were banking on it being successful. All signs looked like this was going to be an even bigger hit than the first record.

On the Saturday after we finished recording, Dean decided he was going to throw an impromptu pool party at his place to celebrate. Everyone and their families were invited, but I had something else planned.

Things between Chase and me had still been weird. Nothing I could put my finger on, and nothing apparent to those around us. He was just… distant. We were so close that the smallest details of our relationship were noticeable to me, and there was definitely something still off.

I had made plans to take him out of the city for the weekend. I had rented a beachfront house in Montauk as a surprise getaway for the two of us. I wanted us to reconnect, smooth over any lingering awkwardness, and enjoy each other's company without any distractions for a few days. He had finished his exams successfully, and we both more than deserved a getaway.

I drove over to his building in my rental car midmorning, marveling at how good it felt to be behind the wheel again. Miraculously, I found a parking spot out front and headed up to his apartment.

"What are you doing here?" he said with a smile, greeting me with a fast kiss as he opened the door.

"I'm here to kidnap you," I replied, fluttering my long eyelashes he had always been envious of. "Pack a bag. You have twenty minutes."

"What?" He looked adorably confused, with an undertone of delight in his eyes.

"We're going away for the weekend. Grab some clothes. You're down to nineteen minutes and thirty seconds." I exaggerated checking the time on my phone for dramatic effect.

"That was so not thirty seconds!" he protested, turning on his heel and dashing down the hall to his bedroom.

He was completely into this, and it gave me a little thrill, making him happy. I followed him, grinning, walking behind him at a normal pace.

By the time I got to his bedroom, he had a duffel bag open on the bed and was grabbing socks and underwear from his dresser. He threw those items into the bag and turned to the closet. I leaned against the doorframe, enjoying watching his thought process on his face.

"Where are we going? I can't do this if I don't know where we're going, Carter!" he called to me, head stuck in the closet as he ruffled through his clothes.

"Nope!" I was enjoying this surprise even more than I'd thought I would. "No hints." I paused for a second. "Bring a bathing suit."

"That's a hint!" He gave me an exasperated look over his shoulder.

But he retrieved a swimsuit, along with a couple pairs of jeans and a few shirts of varying degrees of warmth and formality. He folded them quickly and stuffed them into the bag before darting to the bathroom to fill a Dopp kit.

"Five minutes!" I yelled at him a short time later as he scrambled around in the bathroom.

He jogged back to the bedroom after another minute or so, small zippered bag in his hand. I sauntered over to his closet and looked through it for a second until I located the item I wanted. I threw a pair of flip-flops into his duffel for him, which caused him to raise his eyebrows at me. I leaned over to kiss him on his temple, taking the opportunity to nip his earlobe and whisper, "One minute," into his ear.

He assessed the items in his bag, trying to figure out if he had forgotten anything. A light dawned, and he walked over to his bedside table. He pulled out a strip of condoms with one hand, a small bottle of lube with the other, and looked at me questioningly.

"Absolutely." I nodded solemnly. I had thrown similar items into my own bag at home earlier, but with us, having extra was always a good idea.

He zipped the bag shut as I obnoxiously counted down the timer from ten seconds. Hey, all the *Master Chef* episodes I'd been watching had to have some residual effect; it certainly wasn't going to be improvement in my cooking skills. At zero he collapsed facedown next to his duffel on his bed in exhaustion.

"That was far more difficult than it needed to be," he complained. "You could have told me where we're going."

"Probably. But it's way more fun this way." I swatted his ass playfully. "Come on, we gotta head out."

"Fine." He got up from the bed, pouting, but with a twinkle in his eyes. "Do I even have time to pee first?"

I burst out laughing, shouldering his bag for him and gesturing dramatically for him to go ahead and use the bathroom. This was going to be fun.

Chase

I HAD never been kidnapped before. It mostly seemed stressful. Carter showed up unannounced at my door and gave me less time to pack for a mystery location than any reasonable gay man would need. But I was too wound up to keep grouching for long. He had this habit of surprising me, and as much as I thought I didn't like surprises, his were usually pretty romantic, or at least sexy as hell.

When I saw he had rented a car, I couldn't stop the delight from showing on my face. As with most teenagers, Carter and me getting our driver's licenses was a big deal. He had somehow convinced his parents to buy him a horribly rusty used car for his sixteenth birthday, and some of my best memories from that year before he left were of sitting shotgun driving around town with him, with no direction in mind.

We turned through the streets of lower Manhattan, heading for the freeway. I prodded Carter for clues to our destination, but he was annoyingly tight-lipped. We bickered over radio stations. I finally gave in and let him listen to classic rock after he tried to convince me it was educational, now that I had written that genre of music for his band. Whatever. The weather was beautiful, we were out of the city, and he was whisking me away on a thoughtful getaway. I could live with shitty music on the radio.

We drove for a couple of hours before I had a good sense of our destination, but I kept quiet until we pulled into a long winding driveway, wanting to let him have his surprise.

It was a beautiful secluded beachfront villa. The exterior of the house was a gorgeous coastal blue, with white trim and a wraparound porch complete with a porch swing next to the door. The field in front of the house was filled with purple lavender and delicate wildflowers, all in full bloom. There was no backyard per se, only miles of clear sand and inky blue ocean. Despite the calm day, small waves were visible from where we parked in the drive. The sound of the waves lapping against the shore was rhythmic and immediately calming. A gull cried in the distance. The smell of lavender and saltwater wafted into the car through our open windows. The whole place was like a dream. I grinned at Carter.

"All ours," he said, stepping out of the driver's side door and coming around to get the door for me.

We walked into the gorgeous house hand in hand. The floors were a handsome hardwood, matching the exposed beams in the vaulted ceiling. It had an open floor plan, with the rooms effortlessly flowing into each other. There was a gas fireplace in the living area, surrounded by upholstered couches in the same coastal blue as the exterior. The kitchen had granite countertops and stainless-steel appliances. There was lots of room for cooking, and

I would need to check the cupboards, but it looked like groceries had been left for us too. The whole back wall of the cottage was covered with floor-to-ceiling windows. A sliding glass door adjoined the living room and led to a full patio extending toward the ocean. The patio held a massive barbecue and some furniture on one side and a covered hot tub on the other. Carter's insistence on my bringing my bathing suit was much appreciated when I noticed this, though not having swim shorts would have been fun too!

We wandered farther into the house. It appeared there were at least three bedrooms. We left our bags in the master, which had a handmade wooden bed frame, matching the floors and ceilings. It was as if someone had done all the work on this place by hand. The bedclothes looked soft and inviting, and there was a large abstract painting of a beach and the ocean over the bed. The whole place was heaven. I couldn't decide what I wanted to do first. Carter put his arms around me from behind and kissed my cheek.

"How did you find this place?" I asked, overwhelmed by his sweet gesture of bringing me here.

"Online. I saw the lavender in the front yard in a photo and I was sold," he answered simply.

I gave a contented sigh. "Lavender. I like lavender. There was lavender in the bouquet you gave me too. Before our first date."

"I know you like lavender. You told me that before."

"When did I say that?" I asked. My memory was pretty good, and it surprised me I didn't remember a detail of our relationship over the last few weeks.

"I think it was the summer when we were fourteen. We were camping with our families, and we had gone somewhere on our bikes by ourselves one afternoon."

The memory was old and hazy. I remembered the summer well, and I knew exactly what he was talking about now that he brought it up.

He kept going, lost in the story. "We found this field on a cliff, overlooking the ocean. The field was filled with lavender as far as the eye could see."

I listened, captivated by his side of the narrative.

"We had ditched our bikes, and you had run ahead of me, through all the flowers, with your hands above your head, laughing like crazy. I remember the sun hitting your hair and making it glow. I followed you and caught up eventually. We were so free that day, running together without any care or stress on our minds. When I found you, you had a single perfect stem of lavender in your hand. You told me they were your favorite flower and that you were gay and hoped I would still want to be your friend."

"You put the lavender behind my ear and said of course we were still friends," I said breathlessly, touching the spot in reminiscence. "I can't believe you remember that."

"I remember everything about us, Chase. That moment was special, though, because that was when I knew I was in love with you."

Carter reached out and pulled a small sprig of lavender from a bouquet in a vase on the nightstand. He kissed the spot right over my ear and put the flower in place gently.

HE made love to me slowly and sweetly. I was so ready for him when he entered me that it felt like we were already one. We pushed to get as close together as possible, with every single point of contact our bodies could manage. Our eyes never left one another. Our lips joined until my lungs ached for more air, and when we couldn't kiss, we just breathed each other in. He took me higher than I had ever been, until we could take it no more and finally tumbled together. His name on my lips. My name on his.

Carter

WE spent the afternoon in bed together. Every time with him felt special, but that afternoon was something completely unlike any other. Muscles aching, we finally pulled ourselves away from each other to find food for dinner. I discovered a couple of steaks in the fridge. After throwing a bunch of spices on them, I tossed them on the grill while Chase put together a salad with a bunch of fresh vegetables he found waiting for us. Neither of us were big drinkers, but there were a couple of nice bottles of cabernet stocked in the wine rack, so we decided to celebrate, and I poured us each a glass. We ate outside on the patio, taking in the beautiful view and enjoying each other's company as much as the meal.

The sun started to sink lower in the sky several hours later. We hadn't moved from our spots at the patio table after dinner, preferring to sit and talk long after the meal was done. Between the sound of the ocean, the lingering scent of the lavender, and the fact that I was with my guy, I was perfectly tranquil. Only one thing could possibly make this evening more relaxing.

"What do you say," I started when we had finally moved to the kitchen to clear off our plates, "once we're done with this, we get into that hot tub outside that's calling our names?"

"That sounds—" He kissed me as he brushed past me to put his plate in the dishwasher. "—absolutely wonderful."

I finished up in the kitchen while Chase went to change into the swimsuit I'd insisted he bring. He wandered back into the main room a few minutes later, and fuck, he was so sexy I forgot what I was doing entirely. He had on the same bathing suit I had seen him wearing in the photo I had found months ago online. It was square cut, barely covering the length of his cock and balls and doing absolutely nothing to conceal their shape. The suit was dusty blue, with thin, pale gray stripes running diagonally across his hips. He had a bright pink towel he must have found in a closet somewhere in the house thrown around him, covering just enough of his body to tease that there were still bits of him I couldn't see.

"Not fucking fair," I groaned.

He giggled, playing innocent, and then turned around to give me a view of the most faultless ass in the world. The hem of the shorts only fell half an inch or so below the swell of his cheeks. My mouth went dry. It was a good thing I was standing behind a counter, because my instant hard-on was intense in my jeans.

"Are you absolutely sure you want to go in the hot tub?" I baited him.

"Yes." He moved to stand in front of me. "The hot water is going to feel amazing on my sore muscles."

He picked up my hands from where they rested on the counter and brought them around to his tight round ass, making sure to leave no doubt as to why he was sore.

"I still feel you from earlier. You fucked me so perfectly. God, I love what you do with your cock," he murmured against my lips, taking them swiftly in a fierce kiss. I dragged him against my full groin, my hands never leaving his ass. He pulled back moments later, his lips red and swollen from my kiss.

"Hot tub," he said, unwavering, and moved away from me to make his way outside toward the patio.

"Tease!" I called after him, my groin aching from his antics.

I joined him in the Jacuzzi a few minutes later, pissed at myself for not having thought to purchase a sexier swimsuit to drive him as wild as he had made me. My own suit was longer, wine colored, and fit poorly at the moment because my stubborn cock was still half-hard inside it. I pulled an elastic band off my wrist as I climbed the two stairs to get into the tub, tying my hair into a quick bun to keep it from the water.

"Mmm." His eyes raked over my body.

I certainly didn't look anywhere near as good as he did in his do-me-now bathing suit, but I liked his eyes on me. I sat down beside him, immediately relishing the feel of the hot, silky water on my skin. I pulled him up so he was seated across my lap and began stroking his legs and torso. We sat like that for a while in silence, enjoying the sunset and the feel of each other's bodies.

We crawled into bed a few hours later, serene and happy. Chase was soft, sleepy, and warm, smelling faintly of the appropriately lavender-scented soap. We had finally pulled ourselves out of the hot tub long after the night had fallen and the sky was awash with the bright stars you could never see as well in the city. I fell asleep with him in my arms, knowing in my heart that it might be a tough road, but this was the man I was meant to spend my life with.

Chase

I HAD finished packing the few things I had brought with me to the beach house and was doing a final check to make sure we hadn't forgotten anything. We had spent the second day much the same as the first. Enjoying the time together, relaxing on the deck, and drawing as many orgasms out of each other as we could. We had even gone down to the beach for a while, alternating between walking in the hot sand and in the cool ocean.

I wandered through the sliding door, where Carter was standing with his arms on the railing, looking out at the sea.

"All packed?" he asked me when I walked up alongside him.

"Yup. Are you sure we have to go?" I pouted.

I knew we did. While he was done with the album and had some time off still, I started my summer job the following day. I was actually looking forward to it. I had lucked out and gotten a job helping at the summer music program at Julliard, the one I had attended as a student a million years ago. They only needed a couple of assistants each summer, and the competition was fierce for the positions. It paid well and left enough time in the evenings and weekends for me to keep teaching students privately too. I had one more year before I graduated, and I was determined to get out of school with as little debt hanging over my head as possible. Life wasn't going to be easy for a newly graduated composition major, even if my degree was from Julliard.

"Yeah. We have to head out soon. But that doesn't mean we can't come back. Maybe for a long weekend or something before the end of summer?"

"I'd like that," I said with a smile.

We stood in silence for a moment, watching the waves peacefully crash over the shore.

"Chase, I need to tell you something," Carter said, gripping the railing harder, purposely not looking at me.

My heart sank. I had a feeling I knew what this was about. It was the conversation we had been avoiding for weeks now. I could already feel the tears prickling my eyes. I waited in silence for him to continue.

"They want us to go on tour. They're pushing post for the album to get it done as quickly as possible. They want us in California next week to discuss publicity and a plan, and then we'd leave right after Labor Day. Europe. At least eight months."

I felt sick. The lunch we'd had hours ago threatened to make a reappearance. My pulse raced to the point where I was terrified I was going to have a heart attack. I squeezed my eyes closed, refusing to cry in front of this man whom I loved so much but who was hurting me so deeply. Again. I focused on my breathing. In and out. In and out. My gasps were shaky, but I was taking in oxygen, and that meant I was alive. The waves rushed on, unaware of our momentous conversation. Life kept going on around me, but it felt like time had stopped and my world had been devastated. I felt like I was seventeen again, as helpless as when the boy who owned my heart left me for the first time. Only now I already knew how much it ached to watch him walk away.

I stayed silent.

"Baby, please say something," Carter begged.

I didn't respond. I would fall apart. "How long have you known?" I finally whispered, barely loud enough to be heard over the sea.

"Officially only a couple of hours. Cory texted me this morning. But we had a pretty solid idea a few days ago."

I appreciated his honesty, but it did nothing to ease the sinking feeling in my gut that he was abandoning me all over again. I knew he needed to go. This was a huge career boost for the band, and I wanted to be happy for him. But he'd made me fall for him so hard, only to leave me alone again.

I wanted him in my life. I wanted weekend surprises like this. I wanted skating dates and pizza on the couch and someone to come home to after a shitty day. A boyfriend who was more than the occasional text message, or maybe if we were lucky, a voice on a transatlantic phone call every so often.

My pending senior year was going to be stressful and challenging. I had big decisions to make. Did I want to try to get into a master's program? If so, in what city and at what school? Was I actually cut out to make music for a living? And maybe I didn't need him to make those decisions, but I wanted him to be with me so we could make them together. I wanted to create a life with a partner, and his being away for the better part of a year wasn't compatible with the life I wanted for myself.

"Chase. Please. Talk to me," Carter pleaded.

"I don't want you to go," I said, feeling like an unreasonable child.

He nodded. "I know. I don't want to be apart from you either. I want us to be together more than anything. But this tour—it's huge, Chasey! Amazing cities, venues that are hundreds of years old. Playing my music, *our* music, for people who don't even speak our language. It's the opportunity I've always wanted."

My tears overflowed and started falling slowly at his words. I wanted those things for him. I wanted him to be happy and for him to bring people together with his music. I wanted him to be successful and significant and to change the world through his songs. Our songs.

"I know," I said, echoing him. It was all I could get out.

"I need you to tell me how you feel. I need to know what you're thinking," he said.

I shook my head. My sadness shifted to irritation. At him for being so reasonable and at myself for being too selfish to be happy for him.

"Fine. You want to know how I feel?" I snapped, swiping the tears off my face.

He must have seen my expression transform from hurt to anger. He drew a long breath, as if readying himself for me to lash out at him.

"I feel like this whole weekend was a manipulation. I feel like you brought me here to remember how easy things were when we were kids. The lavender. The beach. To romance me and have sex with me and make me think you were the perfect fucking boyfriend. Only you knew this was coming! You knew it would *fucking* kill me to have you leave me, but you wanted to stick the final nail in the coffin and make me fall *too fucking in love with you* to break up with you before you go!"

I was all but yelling at him now. My tears were flowing freely again—a mix of anger, sadness, and hurt. I hated him for leaving. I hated myself for hating him for leaving. I wanted him to leave now so it would just be over. I wanted him to hold me and never let me go. I was a complete and total mess.

"You're right." He nodded slowly. "I did want to make us both remember how far we've come and how good we are. I want nothing more than to be with you, Chase. But I don't want you to be miserable and lonely in return. I love you. I've loved you since I was fourteen. I will love you for the rest of my life. Unquestionably. Eight months isn't a long time when I want forever. But if it's too much for you, I get it."

"I hate that you're putting this on me. It's not fair, C. You're making yourself come off as the martyr, and yet I'm the one that has to pull the trigger, even though this is fucking killing me!"

"You're wrong, Chase," he said, trying to calm me down and not agitate me further. "The easy thing would be for me not to go. Is that what you want? It would be suicide, Chase. It would destroy the band I've worked for years to build. It would ruin my reputation with the biggest label in the country. I'm not good at anything else, baby! This is it for me. Music. Is. It. For. Me. It's my only option. But if it means losing you…."

"What, C! If it means losing me, what?" I cried. Hating myself for not immediately insisting he go. Hating that I was even considering forcing him to make that choice. Hating that I must be the most selfish asshole on the entire fucking planet.

"I don't know," he said, and the heartrending honesty I couldn't fault him for utterly crushed me.

Carter

THE ride home was horrible. We were both silent for the entire drive. We literally didn't say one word to each other. I didn't know what was happening or what his silence meant. His face was turned away from me toward the window the whole time. I would glance over occasionally, seeing his broken expression reflected in the glass. Every so often, he would sniff lightly, or I would see his hand reach up to brush a fallen tear from his cheek, and my heart would break all over again. With the exception of my family moving away in high school, I had never felt more helpless in my life.

I honestly didn't know what to do. There wasn't a simple solution. The romantic side of my brain, the side that would do anything for him, wanted to throw all the other crap out the window and do whatever it took to be with him. But life wasn't that easy. I had a contract, a legal obligation to the label to uphold. And even if I didn't, was I prepared to walk out on the band? Beau, Ash, and Dean had gone through hell with me for the past couple of years. It wouldn't just destroy my dreams, but theirs as well. It would be next to impossible for any of us to get work in this business if we broke the contract. I loved what I did. The growing success of the Thorns? It meant the world to me. But Chase…. Chase was the love of my life. I knew it more each day. Losing him was not an option either.

It would have been so easy to be frustrated with him, to think of him as selfish and greedy and inconsiderate. But Chase was none of those things. He was only hurt by this because he wanted to be with me so badly, and how could anyone not be flattered by that? He knew what he wanted, and he had been honest about that from the beginning. More and more it seemed like this one impasse was an insurmountable obstacle, but I wasn't willing to let either Chase or the band go.

We hit traffic coming into the city, adding a new level of misery to the end of the drive. Eventually we made our way off the freeway, over the bridge, and through the streets of lower Manhattan. I stopped the car outside his building. He didn't make a move to get out, so I took that as an opportunity to risk breaking the silence.

"I love you, Chase," I said simply.

"I love you too."

"What happens now?" I pleaded for any reassurance he could give me. Any indication that this wouldn't be a catastrophic stalemate we couldn't recover from.

"I don't know. I need to get my head on straight and figure out what I want. How you fit into that. Go to California. When you get back, we'll talk."

As much as I desperately wanted him to say, "Fuck it, we're worth the separation and everything will be okay," I appreciated his wanting to take some time to think. I genuinely did want him to be happy, instead of placating me and then being miserable and breaking up with me later anyway. He had always been the more mature of the two of us.

"Okay," I agreed. "I love you." I needed him to not just hear the words again but to understand how much I truly meant them.

"I love you too," he echoed, but his voice was hollow. He opened the door, grabbed his bag from the back seat, and headed for the walkway to his building.

Carter

I FOUGHT the urge to text Chase throughout my time in LA. I respected him enough to give him space, and I didn't want to complicate his life or upset him any more than I already had. At least daily, I saw something that made me think of him. A community piano on the street, lavender flowers in a florist shop, a kitschy diner with horrible wallpaper. I wanted to tell him about my day, hear how working at the Julliard summer program was going. I wanted to remind him that I loved him. There was a beautiful moment each morning when I first woke up and hadn't yet remembered we were in this awful fight. I would wake up with a smile on my face, thinking how happy I would be to see him or talk to him that day. Then the horrible realization would hit me that it wasn't going to happen, and the pain came on hard and fast all over again.

The band noticed that something had changed in me too. They went from joking around with me like usual to avoiding talking to me after I'd snapped some angry remark at each of them one time too many. I was convinced Cory was going to tell me off for being a liability with his bosses and fucking this up for all of us. But he didn't. I sat with my arms crossed through consultations, staying largely silent and only grumbling out responses when I couldn't get out of talking. The fact that I had to listen to the songs Chase and I had written together about a hundred thousand times didn't help my attitude either.

With one day of meetings left to go in California, the band staged an impromptu intervention. They had invited me to go to a bar with them again. And I had said no again. With no excuse again. It was a few minutes after nine, and I was already getting ready for bed. I had been depressed as fuck, having no energy for days and seeing no purpose in either going out with them or staying awake by myself. I debated not answering when they knocked at my hotel room door, but then they started shouting at me, and it was more trouble to fight it than to pretend to listen to whatever lecture they were going to give me.

I pulled open the door and gazed out at the three of them standing in a semicircle. I was wearing only a pair of old sleep pants, so I waited until they grabbed the door from me and walked into my room before pulling on a shirt. I sat cross-legged on the foot of the king-size bed, ready for them to tell me I was a terrible person who was letting down the team.

Dean cut right to the chase. No pun intended. "What's going on, Cart?"

He grabbed the rolling desk chair from the corner and moved it so he could sit directly across from me.

Beau settled himself on the bed beside me, and Ash leaned against the wall, all three ready to do battle.

"You've been in a shit mood all week when these guys are literally handing us a European tour on a silver platter," Dean continued.

I stared at him dead-eyed, not caring what he accused me of.

"Carter." Beau put his hand on my knee, trying a different approach. "Did something happen with you and Chase?"

"What is this—fucking good cop, bad cop?" I accused, shifting until Beau took his hand off me.

"We want to help, C. How can—"

"Do *not* call me that!" I cut Beau off violently, practically snarling at him.

Beau inhaled deeply.

"Well, at least we're sure what the problem is now," Dean muttered.

"Shut the fuck up, Dean," I snapped.

Beau frowned and shook his head. "Dean, not helping." Then, with more force behind it than before, "Carter, what happened?"

"You know what's wrong. Can you all fuck off now? I'm tired, and I wanna go to bed." I moved to get under the covers, turning on my side to face away from them and hide the sudden tears that were threatening to fall yet again.

I was so fucking tired of crying. Tired of barely getting through the day. Tired of not knowing what was going to happen and being terrified I was going to lose Chase. That I had already lost him. I closed my eyes and feigned sleep until the guys finally gave up and left me alone.

Chase

I WAS miserable. The first few days after the ill-fated Montauk trip, it was all I could do to get through the day. I tried to enjoy the experience of working at the summer program, but it felt like a façade. I could barely get my mind off Carter. I wondered if he was thinking about me. Were his meetings going well? Was he as miserable as I was? More than once I needed to feign a visit to the bathroom in the middle of the day to pull myself together when my emotions had gotten the best of me.

I missed him desperately, but I didn't have a solution to our problem. If I missed him this much now, what would it be like for eight months? Or next time, if it was a world tour that lasted a year or more? How would I deal with that? Could we ever have a house together? A dog? Kids someday, maybe? The jury was still out on whether

I wanted that last one or not, but not at least having it on the table? Raising children was something I would never want to do without a permanent partner.

Eli pulled me aside when we were packing up after Friday's session. He was one of the lead instructors for the piano students, and we were paired together a lot. Normally I relished working with Eli; we got along, and he always had insightful advice for the students. But he knew me well enough to see something was wrong faster than any of the other instructors would have.

"Is everything okay, Chase? You've been off this week. Are you not enjoying the job?" he asked me.

"The job's great." I forced a smile.

"It's something, though."

"Nothing. Nonwork stuff. I'll try harder to focus. Please don't fire me." I was a little nervous that this was more serious than I thought. I wasn't prepared to lose my job this early in the summer.

"Whoa, relax," he said. "Nothing like that at all. I just care about you and want to make sure you're okay."

I gave a small sigh of relief, thinking that would be the end of the conversation.

But Eli was not letting the subject drop. "Is it about that guy you told me about? From when you were young?"

I tensed, turned my back on him, and made a show of focusing on stacking the chairs so the janitors could vacuum the floor.

Eli put his hand on my back to stop me. He sat in the chair next to the one I was getting ready to clear, gesturing for me to join him.

I sat beside him. After a second, I exhaled.

"Carter. His name is Carter West," I started. "He's the lead singer for the band Inevitable Thorns."

Eli raised his eyebrows but remained quiet, allowing me to continue.

"We've been dating for the last couple of months. Well, I guess dating is a mild description for it, but we're together. He's away now for a week to plan an eight-month European tour with his band. We had a horrible fight before he left. I don't know how to deal. It feels like I'm not being supportive, but I really can't function without him. I want to be strong, but I'm so fucking weak. These last few days have proven that. I just can't do it."

Eli paused, digesting my brain dump.

"Are you upset about him being gone or about the fight?" Eli asked.

"Both. I miss him. I miss talking to him. I hate how we left things. I want to be happy that he has this massive opportunity, but I can't get over how it affects me and our relationship. It's selfish, I know, but I can't help it." I considered what I'd said, checking that it was the truth.

"Well, you miss him because you're not talking to him. Not seeing him is one thing, but not texting? Calling? Skyping? At least if you were together when he's gone, you would have something." Eli stated it like it was obvious.

I mumbled my agreement. He was right; I'd give him that.

"I asked you before if he was worth it," Eli said. "Worth dealing with the absences to be with him. It sounds like you're leaning more toward thinking he's not worth it?"

I thought about it. Really thought about it. A loop played in my mind—different memories from the past couple of months. Moments between us. Big conversations. Passing glances. Surprises. Songwriting. I smiled fondly at the images in my brain.

"Chase, I don't want to tell you what to do, but you seem pretty miserable right now without him," Eli continued, unaware of the path of my internal thoughts.

"I do. I do want to be with him," I said, starting slowly and finishing with the words flying from my mouth.

I didn't know how true it was until the words were already out. I wanted to be with him. It *was* worth it. This argument? This avoiding each other? This was what was awful. I thought back to the silent ride home from Montauk. Being in a relationship but not physically being with him seemed way better than sitting side by side without talking.

"I have to go. I'll be back in a minute." I ran out of the room to find an empty office or studio somewhere where I could call him.

I pulled my phone out of my pocket and dialed Carter's number. It went straight to voicemail.

Carter

I PULLED my head out of my ass long enough to get through Friday's meetings. The guys left me alone. I started to consider how I had acted toward them. We were a team. We had been through a lot together, and I was sure they were freaking out about what it would mean if something were to happen to the lead singer and songwriter when shit was starting to get serious.

The plan was basically set for the tour. The album would be done in a few weeks and would be released in the middle of August. We would do a crap ton of publicity for it, mainly in New York, but also back in LA. Talk shows, magazines, the whole thing. For our first album release, we had been a bunch of nobodies, so having people care about our album before even hearing it was all new to us. The tour would run from September through till April or May. We were hitting all the major cities, and a few strategic smaller markets as well. London, Berlin, Rome, Madrid. Paris. That one stung a little. I had dreamed of seeing the Eiffel Tower with Chase. It felt like so long ago. Another lifetime.

Along with Cory, they were hiring us a full-time sound technician who would tour with us, as well as a merch seller and a bus driver. We were playing bigger venues than we had on the US tour and had more time off between shows, so more nights would be spent in hotels than on the bus. The label was petrified about me blowing my voice out due to the complexity of the music on this album.

The meetings were all completed by noon. All hands had been shaken; all venue contracts were underway. I caught Beau's arm when we were heading out, gesturing to him to follow me over to a park bench in the landscaped garden of the label's office. It was time for me to man up. First with Beau and then hopefully with Chase once I was back in New York. I needed to face the music, so to speak, and deal with whatever his decision was like an adult.

"I wanted to apologize," I started when Beau and I were seated. "I've been in a crappy mood all week, and I know you guys were just trying to help."

Beau made a noncommittal sound of agreement, then asked again, "What's going on, Carter?"

"Chase and I had a fight. He's not sure if he can deal with me being away for so long on tour. I don't know what's going to happen with us, but I've been a shitty bandmate at a really important time for us, and that hasn't been fair. I'll do better, I promise." I tried to be stronger on the outside than I felt internally.

"Oh, Cart. I'm sorry. That must have been so hard listening to the album all week too." Beau's understanding and sympathy were more than I deserved.

"Not easy, yeah," I agreed. "But I want him to be happy, and I know it's a rough life for a partner to have to deal with. I'm gonna talk to him when I get home. See what he wants to do."

"But you want to be with him?"

"Of course I do. He's amazing. He's smart and funny. He's caring and kind and passionate. He's sexy as hell, but so cute and sweet too. And I literally have no idea how we'll ever put together an album as good as this one without him. He's a fucking genius with music, and we've never sounded this good before." I was gushing by that point, my heart swelling with each phrase in memory of my guy.

"So work with that," Beau said. "Hire him. Have him write for us. He can tour, same as Cory or the new mix or the merch girl. The guys love him, and you're right, he's the reason why this album is as good as it is."

I froze.

"Holy shit!" My heart flew into high gear. It was such a simple solution.

"We should hire him," I breathed, putting all the pieces together in my mind.

He could work for us. We traveled with enough backline that he could have a keyboard or whatever else he needed. He could write when we were in rehearsals or sound check, in the bus, at hotels. We would have the same schedule and could be together on tour. If he wanted to write for theater or pop musicians or whatever, he could do that too. Hell, we could even introduce him to some artists who would buy his pieces. He was so good the world deserved to hear his music. We already knew our label liked his stuff; it probably wouldn't take much convincing to get them to agree to let him travel with us. Wouldn't even cost them an extra hotel room.

"Beau, I need to go." I stood suddenly on shaky legs.

I ran across the garden to jump into my rental car and head to LAX as quickly as possible. I heard Beau laughing at me all the way across the parking lot.

"Apologize to Dean and Ash for me!" I yelled at him over his amusement.

Carter

I LANDED back in New York just after ten o'clock. I hadn't been sleeping properly, and even with the time change, I was exhausted. As soon as the plane landed, I switched my phone out of airplane mode. I had a number of texts, including one from Beau and one from Dean, both wishing me luck. God, I owed the band a proper explanation and a full apology. I made a mental note to take them to dinner or something once everyone was back in town. And Beau, well, if his plan worked, he could have my kingdom.

I checked the missed call I had and realized it was from Chase. My stomach did a flip-flop. There was no voicemail or text from him, so he must have tried my phone when I was in the air. My anxiety went wild, not knowing if it was good or bad news he was calling with. We hadn't had a formal plan about what would happen when I got back from LA besides the loose agreement to talk. I couldn't even remember if I'd told him officially when I was getting back.

The deplaning process took approximately five years. As soon as I was off the plane and on the ramp, I started sprinting around the other passengers, looking for a corner or someplace quiet to call him. I probably looked like a crazy person and crossed my fingers that nobody would recognize me at that particular moment. I saw a room marked Employees Only and tried the door. Fortunately it was unlocked, and there was nobody inside. It was a small storage closet, but that was more than okay with me.

I took a second when I had Chase's number on the screen, trying to even out my breaths and work up the courage to start the call. I hit the button.

The phone rang three times before he picked up.

"Carter?" he asked, sounding disoriented. I'd thought it would still be early enough that he wouldn't have been asleep, but maybe I was wrong.

"Hey, Chase, it's me. Listen, I saw that you called, but I was on a plane. Back to New York. I'm in New York. I just landed." I sounded like a moron, but he hadn't hung up yet, so I kept rambling. "I'm not sure what you wanted to say, but I need to talk to you. In person. Please don't say no. Can I come now? Or tomorrow if that's better for you? Please. I really need to talk to you."

"Yeah, C. Now is good. Are you hungry? I can order us some food."

"Sure? I just want to see you. Beyond that is up to you. I'll be there in less than an hour, okay? I've just gotta get my bag and then I'll hop in a cab."

I was so relieved that he hadn't shot me down. That had to be a good sign, right?

"Okay. I'll see you then," Chase agreed.

"I still love you, Chase. I'll be there soon," I told him, and then, like the coward I was, I hung up the phone before he could respond.

Chase

I WAS asleep when Carter called. Pathetic, I know, as it wasn't even ten thirty on a Friday evening. But it had been an emotionally exhausting week between our fight and starting work, so I figured a little self-care and an early night were called for. I did a quick sweep of my apartment when I hung up the phone. I wasn't a messy person by nature, but then again, the fraught week hadn't left me a lot of energy to put things away properly. After tidying my hair a little, I threw on a comfortable pair of jeans and a V-neck light green T-shirt. The Chinese food I ordered showed up about ten minutes before Carter said he expected to be here, so I got some plates and cutlery ready and left it all on the kitchen counter.

A knock at the door a few minutes later made my heart pound. As much as I was unsure about how this conversation was going to go, I was more excited to see him than anything. God, I had missed him. I opened the door, and the most attractive man in the world was standing in front of me. He looked so good. He was dressed simply—basic jeans and a black T-shirt with his signature black leather bomber jacket. He had a suitcase behind him, and his expression was one of concern, but he couldn't school the grin that broke out when I opened the door. He opened his arms tentatively, and I had a sudden flashback to him opening his dressing-room door with the same gesture at the Radio City show so many months ago. I went to him willingly, melting into his arms. My head still fit so perfectly under his chin. His pine aftershave was faint but still did crazy things to my senses. I never wanted him to let me go. I was getting seriously emotional from a simple hug, so I was mildly relieved when he released his hold on me.

"Hey, Chase." He smiled hesitantly.

"Hi, C." I matched the look he was giving me without thinking about it.

I moved away from the doorframe, giving him room to manipulate his suitcase through the door.

"I ordered some Chinese food. I wasn't sure if you would have eaten or not," I said.

It was so much easier to deflect. I was too much of a coward to jump right into the awkward conversation we needed to have.

"I could eat," he told me.

I served us each a helping, using forks, not chopsticks, and saying a silent apology to Chinese culture. Neither of us said anything. Probably neither of us knew how to read the other. After a bite or two, he sighed, pushing the food around his plate, and began.

"I've been thinking a lot while I was gone. I hate how we left things. I've been moody and miserable and a pain in the ass to deal with."

I smiled at his self-deprecating words, knowing exactly what a brooding Carter was like from our teenage years. It was also exactly the same way I had been feeling the past week, so I completely understood what he was getting at.

"I don't want to lose you," he went on. "I want to fight for you, for us, because you're all I've wanted since I was fourteen years old. I know deep down you feel it too. We've come back from worse than this in the past. We are *meant* to be together. You're it for me, Chase case. You're the one. And whatever it takes to make that happen, however I need to show you that I love you, I want to do that."

He was staring at me intently, emotion leaking from behind his eyes and through his speech, which felt both well-rehearsed and completely spontaneous. I believed him. I knew what he was feeling because I felt it too. This was forever between us. I stayed quiet, letting him go on.

"I understand that my life is difficult. I know it's going to be hard, and you're the one making more of the sacrifices here. I want to prove to you that it's worth it. And I think I have a solution for the long-term. It's a little bit unconventional, but when have we ever been ordinary?"

I was intrigued. It meant a lot to me that he was acknowledging my internal battle with all of this instead of shrugging it off and saying I would have to deal with him being gone.

"What's the solution?" I asked, absorbed in his words.

"Beau and I were talking. I was being an asshole all week, and he called me on it. I gave him the outline of what happened." He paused uncertainly. "I hope that was okay."

I nodded encouragement, and he went on. I couldn't judge him for going to Beau, considering I went to Eli in much the same way.

"Beau pointed out how important you had become to the Thorns. How it's your work that's on our album and what's going to make the record a hit. I know it wouldn't be the picket fence all the time, but what if you were to tour with us? Like, we hired you to write our music? We would travel with all the keyboards and gear you would need anyway. You seemed to like the guys and the stuff we were working on, and they love working with you. You're way too good for a crappy internship that pays next to nothing. You're a composer, Chase. Your music deserves to be heard." Carter picked up speed and enthusiasm as he blathered on.

A smile broke out on my face. He took that as encouragement and kept going.

"I know you still have a year of school left. But that's such a small amount of time. We could talk every day. I could fly home to see you when we have a couple days off. You could come spend Christmas with us. We'll be in Paris over Christmas. Wouldn't that be amazing? And at the end of the year, we'll be done being apart. I want to negotiate longer breaks between tours. We need more time to write and rest than we had this time. Maybe we could get a house or something. Live where we want. You could write—for us, for other bands. We have connections and can help. I know it's not exactly your style, but what we did together is fucking good. Please think about it at least?" He finally went quiet, looking at me intently.

"I don't need to think about it. It makes complete sense. Working on your album was incredible. I want to be with you, C. And yes, I wanted the house and the dog… but if this is how we get to be together, it's perfect."

Carter's plan was too good to be true. The solution was obvious, now that I thought about it. It might not be exactly my dream scenario, but it sounded like a hell of an adventure too. I had already made up my mind that Carter was worth everything. If we saw each other all the time it seemed more plausible for us to be together long-term.

"Really? Are you sure?" He was so adorably exhilarated, maybe still not quite believing my words but hoping I meant what I'd said.

"Yeah. Completely. I want you. Us. This makes sense. As long as we have time between being on the road. I want a life outside that too, but it sounds like this is the right thing for all of us." I remained calm on the outside, but on the inside I was a million bouncing rubber balls, alive with possibility and jumping frantically in every direction.

His reaction was immediate. He let out a loud whoop and dashed to my side of the kitchen island to pick me up and spin me around. I laughed loudly, unencumbered by any more fear or doubt. I threw my head back and felt a weight lift off my shoulders, replaced by the sudden, absolute joy I had been missing for so long. I bent my knees, letting him twirl me, holding on to him for all I was worth. He finally let me down, his hands staying on my waist.

"Promise?" he asked, but he already knew the answer. I could tell from the huge grin on his face, a look of pure happiness.

"I promise."

He leaned into me slowly, enjoying the moment and making sure I wanted this as much as he did. His hands on my hips, his breath against me. He nuzzled my cheeks, my jaw, relishing getting to touch me.

"I love you, Chase," he murmured against my skin.

All the cells in my body were awake and attuned to what he was doing. The synapses in my brain were firing in overdrive. My heart was simultaneously in my throat and had broken open, overwhelmed by how much love I felt in this moment.

"I love you too," I whispered back, barely getting the words out before he took my lips in a fervent kiss.

Carter's lips were perfect, and the pressure of them against my mouth was intoxicating. Taking control of my bottom lip, he sucked it into his mouth. He licked along it, stimulating nerve endings I didn't even know I had. He teased the corners of my mouth, making me gasp and open up for him. Carter took the opportunity to plunge his tongue inside, rubbing the bottom of my tongue, exploring every corner and crevice.

I ran my hands up and down his chest over his shirt, savoring the touch I hadn't been sure I would get again, reacquainting myself with every muscle and ridge. He rubbed his fingers over my hip bones, holding me tightly. His hips started to rock subtly against mine, craving friction. My cock was swollen and heavy, eager to be reunited with his body.

"Wait, wait," he gasped, pulling his lips from mine but keeping our hips touching. "Are you sure you're sure about this?"

"Yes. Positive. Promise." I pressed my erection into his, felt the heat of his arousal radiating through all the layers of clothing between us. "Please, Carter, I need you. We're good. I need you."

Carter

I TOOK his lips again in a fever. Desperation grew inside me. My cock was so hard for him I thought it might burst through my jeans. I'd missed his lean body. Missed his tight, warm ass. Missed tasting his seed as he came down my throat.

The urge to get him naked and fuck him pulled at me. But one other impulse was stronger. I wanted—no, I needed—to feel him inside of me instead. We had talked about it before but had never actually followed through. Our mutual love of me taking him, forcing myself inside him and making him scream and shake with pleasure, was generally what we both ended up begging for when we fucked.

My hole clenched with need at my train of thought.

"Want you in me. Please. Will you fuck me this time?" I pleaded.

"Oh fuck. Fuck!" Chase cried with a shudder.

I took that as a positive sign he was into the idea. He tilted his head, and I took full advantage by sucking on the spot I adored where his neck met his shoulder.

"Yes?" I asked, needing to know he was on board for this.

"Fuck. Yes. Now. Please," he gasped, pulling me toward his bedroom, already reduced to single words.

"Gonna need you to walk me through this," I said, dragging him back against me when the bedroom door closed behind us.

"Okay. I can do that." He nodded, appearing a bit tentative. Then his eyes sparkled mischievously. "Step one: take your pants off." We both cracked up, which broke some of the tension.

"Thanks, that's super helpful," I said, nipping his lower lip as I stretched one arm around his back and pulled up the bottom of his shirt while softly stroking the skin on his stomach with my other hand.

I kissed him again, his expression switching from jovial to lustful in a heartbeat. Once he was pliant and needy in my arms, I took a step back, making sure his gaze was on my fingertips as I slowly unbuttoned my jeans. His teeth sank into his bottom lip, and a moan escaped as the denim dropped to the floor. I met his stare, cupping my very full package through my black briefs, wanting to draw more of those sexy-as-fuck sounds from him.

I slid my jacket over my arms, keeping the impromptu strip show going. He groaned again, raising his right hand to his dick to give it a small squeeze through his pants. I moved his hand away, though.

"None of that, now," I said.

I ran my hand down his front, undid the button of his jeans, and pulled down the zipper. Then I slid the fabric over his hips, leaving us both in only our underwear and shirts. I moved my mouth next to his ear at the same time as I reached for his dick and leisurely stroked it a couple of times.

"That's all for me," I whispered, directly into his ear.

He made a broken sound, his cock twitched in my hand, and a wet patch formed on his red boxer briefs as he leaked precome.

"Then you better let it go if you want it anywhere other than in your hand," he said, shaking.

I smiled at him innocently. "You know I do."

I let go of his length and stripped off both of our shirts in quick succession, needing to feel his chest against mine. I pulled my briefs down slowly, letting him have a good look as I stepped out of them.

"Fuck, C," he said with reverence, staring at my body and doing great things for my ego.

He reached out to stroke me, fingers soaring over my skin and making me arch into his touch. I closed my eyes, wanting to soak in the feeling of his hands on me.

"Have you… have you ever done this with anything be-before? F-fingers? Toys?" he asked without meeting my eyes, playing with the hair on my chest.

"Fingers," I told him, unembarrassed to admit my personal explorations. "But not in a while."

"That's okay. We'll go slow. Want it to be good for you," he said, seeming almost in a trance watching his hands on me.

I led him to the bed, stopping to retrieve supplies from his nightstand. I lay on my back, pulling him atop me, not a doubt in my mind I was ready to do this with him. He kissed me, and I saw stars. I knew I wanted to be with my Chase as close as we could get. I wanted to let him into my body. He was already inside my heart.

He reached for the lube and squirted the slick liquid onto his fingers. He kissed down my chest, encouraging me to spread my legs for him. He was eye level with my cock now, but my erection had flagged a little from nerves. I wasn't normally one to be body conscious, but it made me feel so exposed having him down there, looking at the most private part of me.

"Just breathe, C. If it's not good for you, we'll stop. I promise."

He gently separated my asscheeks with one hand while sneaking his fingers in with the other to rub up and down my crack. I was tense. I was sure he could feel it. I tried to relax, but my body was fighting me.

"Just breathe," he repeated like a mantra, keeping up the soft caress with his fingers.

He finally grazed over my hole with the tip of one fingernail. My whole body seized up, rigid against my will. It was only a matter of getting started, I was sure. Once the endorphins kicked in, I had liked playing there with my fingers in the past. Chase was reading my body language like a book. He backed off for a second and tried another tactic.

He licked slowly over my half-deflated cock, jolting me quickly back to full mast. I had missed his talented mouth while I was gone. He sucked the head between his waiting lips with a pop, circling it over and over with his tongue until I was a needy mess under him, moaning and making sounds that only he could pull from me.

I barely noticed his finger circling the outer muscles of my hole anymore—until I did. Actually, now that I was paying attention, it felt fucking good to have his finger there. He worked me from both sides until I was squirming beneath him.

He pushed one finger into me to the first knuckle. He pressed it in slowly, a millimeter at a time, his lips still on my cock. When the finger was fully inside, he started slowly pumping it in and out, until I was pushing back for more. By the time he added a second finger, it felt so good that I had to beg him to stop blowing me, knowing I was too close to coming from that alone.

He pulled off my dick with one last mind-blowing suck, leaving me wet and leaking against my stomach. His fingers were making me crazy, opening me up for his gorgeous cock. I felt him grinding his hips into the bed, so turned on from what he was doing to me that he was practically humping the mattress. I lost control over my mouth, my jaw limp and open, sounds coming out that I had no idea I could make. It was so damn good. I never wanted this to end, and at the same time I wanted him to speed up and get to the main event.

Chase reached beside me, adding some more lube to his hand, slicking up a third finger. The stretch was intense with three digits. It burned a little when they first entered me, but the burn quickly faded into that same inconceivable pleasure. He drove in and out of my ass until I couldn't take it anymore.

"Please… now…" was all I could pant out, amazed that I could even remember those simple words.

Chase nodded at me, agreeing that I was prepped enough for him. He slipped his boxer briefs down over his hips, his cock leaving a string of precome on the fabric as he took them off. He slid the foil wrapper off the bed stand and opened it quickly, then rolled the condom over his deep red cock, hissing as his fingers made contact with the aching flesh.

"Tell me… what you're feeling. If you w-want me to stop," he reminded me, his voice thick with arousal and emotion as he covered the condom with more lube.

"Don't stop," I whispered as I guided him to my entrance.

He squeezed his eyes closed, pushing gently but consistently against the tight ring of muscles. I kept forgetting he had never been at this end of things either, since he seemed so confident and self-assured. I supposed it was from knowing what he liked in my position. My body fought him a little, but I breathed and tried to stay loose for him.

The tip pushed inside me, making me gasp. It felt nothing like his fingers. Not unpleasant, exactly, just an intense stretch. Chase let out a moan above me and drove in a little farther. He sank into my body slowly, making the sexiest sounds I'd ever heard, telling me how good I felt, how tight I was, how much he loved me.

His cock filled me up completely. When he was in, he stilled, letting us both adjust. It was the most beautifully deep pressure. I had never felt so close to him and never wanted him to leave my body. He fucked me gently, unhurried, as if to make sure I was still doing okay time and time again. The tenderness tore me apart inside; the care he was showing for me broke me to my core. He held me and kissed me, worshipping my body in every way he knew how.

On one stroke, he found what must have been my prostate. My vision went white, and I cried out, never having felt that before. He hit that spot again and again, making me squeeze my eyes closed with pleasure until tears ran down my cheeks. He brushed them away, kissing me tenderly but fucking into me unrelentingly.

He told me I was beautiful, that he was sorry, that he never wanted us to be apart. That he was so close. The last words were followed immediately with a hard, perfect thrust, and I came with stars shooting behind my eyelids, neither of us having touched my cock since I took him inside me. I shot and shot and shot, shaking and yelling until my throat was raw. His body tensed above me, and he fucked his orgasm into me as hard as he could while my ass spasmed around him.

I opened my eyes to stare up at him when the worst of the tremors had finally passed. His cheeks were stained with tears too. He leaned down to kiss my gasping lips, his cock still buried inside me. We kissed for a long time, having shared something for the first time together that could never be taken away from us.

"Did you just come untouched from me fucking you?" he breathed with astonishment when we finally separated.

"A little bit." I tried to make it a joke, biting back a laugh at his sincerity.

"Holy fuck," he swore. "We're fucking doing that again."

I laughed, agreeing with him wholeheartedly.

Carter

Six months later

I STOOD at the Arrivals gate at Charles De Gaulle Airport, a bouquet of fragrant lavender and bright purple lilacs in hand. It was December fifteenth, ten days before Christmas, and Chase's plane had landed half an hour ago.

We had been apart for a few months now. I was able to sneak a couple of days off in October to visit him, but that was it. I missed him fiercely. Despite the distance, things had been going well for us. We had been talking every day, and while it was hard not to see each other face-to-face, our conversations were real, and we kept each other involved. There were times when he struggled. Hell, there were times we both struggled, but it never felt not worth it. The days until the end of his semester and my tour were numbered. This was temporary.

The band had negotiated for most of the following summer off. We would play a handful of local festival gigs, but we all wanted more time to ourselves after being so busy lately. Our album hit the charts hard. It was well received by critics and fans alike, and the European tour had been a smashing success so far. Grammy nominations came out last week, and Chase and I had cried on the phone together when we learned we had been nominated for our work. The band was stoked, and it was even more motivation for us to keep working together.

Chase was doing well in school in his final year. He had decided not to enter a master's program anytime soon and had a verbal contract with our management team that would be finalized at some point when we decided it was time to record again. He kept his Brooklyn apartment, despite my constant insistence that he should live in my bigger place closer to his school. His determination to make his own way could be frustrating, when all I wanted to do was spoil him, but I ultimately respected him more for his independence. Besides, we were already talking about renting the lavender house for the summer, and I was fairly confident I could convince him to move in with me by fall.

As I watched the automatic doors open for the hundredth time, I caught a glimpse of him in the distance. He was walking toward me through the crowd. His hair was a little longer, and he had a jacket on that I didn't recognize, but it was absolutely my Chase. He spotted me, a grin breaking out, and he started walking faster. I moved as close as I could to the doors, my arms wide and my heart full. We fell into each other, and all was right again. We fit so easily, so naturally, into each other's lives, there was no question in my mind that this incredible man would be next to me forever.

Keep reading for an excerpt from
Dance with Me
by Veronica Cochrane
Inevitable Duets: Book Two

Beau

"**YOU** play keyboard most of the time, even when there's a full grand piano on the stage. Why?" Some preppy, glasses-and-button-down-wearing student in the middle asked me with his eyes full of condescension.

I thought about the question for a second, wanting to be honest about my answer but not blatantly insulting to all of the classically trained musicians in the lecture hall. I had agreed to talk to some freshmen as a favor to Chase, a good friend of mine who was an upperclassman in music composition at the Juilliard School. I never liked interviews much to begin with, and I had known going into this thing that my style of playing would be vastly different from what these kids were used to. The students at these types of private conservatories always seemed to have their noses in the air; however, Chase was adamant that the professor wanted to showcase the variety of career paths one could take in the music industry. I respected that, and seeing how Chase was basically the reason I wasn't a washed-up has-been before my twenty-fifth birthday, I was more than amenable to helping out when he approached me. That and I didn't have anything better to do today.

"Um, I guess it just suits me better? I'm not a classical pianist by any stretch of the imagination, and sitting behind a grand doesn't feel right to me most of the time," I answered. "There are a couple songs either Carter or I will play on the piano, but normally the keyboard is a better fit for me and also for our sound."

I was introduced to Chase through his boyfriend, my bandmate Carter West, earlier in the year. When our band, Inevitable Thorns, got back from our first national tour last spring, we struggled to write new music for our sophomore record. The four members of our group shared the songwriting responsibility, but we were all exhausted and were feeling the pressure to create music that lived up to the first release. We were ridiculously lucky that Chase came into our lives and stepped up, cowriting most of the songs that made the final cut. The album was absurdly well received, and our label immediately arranged for us to embark on an eight-month European circuit. A little over two months into the tour, it was going incredibly well, and we were having the time of our lives. However, we still faced some challenges.

Which is why we were here in New York now. Three days between gigs and Carter insisted upon hiring a private plane to fly us all across the Atlantic so he could see his guy. Carter was noticeably smitten with Chase, and fortunately it seemed like Chase was equally infatuated with Carter. It was sweet, really. They were perfect together, and I was exceedingly happy for them, yet seeing them so googly-eyed about each other made me wonder if I was missing out on something.

A couple more hands shot up, but the professor thankfully cut them off before I was forced to answer any more questions.

"I think that's all we have time for today. Thanks so much to Beau Davis for finding an hour in his busy schedule to join us. Class, remember your midterm paper is due in two weeks. Do *not* leave this one to the last minute."

The students shuffled—putting away notebooks and laptops, chatting with their neighbors as they left. I stuck around, and the professor and I made small talk for a minute or two. He began to pack up his things, so I thanked him again and headed for the exit. As I entered the adjoining hallway, I looked out the windows to see that it was absolutely pissing down rain outside. When Chase had walked me in, we'd entered through a hidden door in the courtyard that was right next to the classroom. Chase had already finished his classes and left, taking advantage of the few hours he had remaining with Carter.

I decided to cut through a hallway that looked like it led in the opposite direction, attempting to exit the building closer to the street, where I could hopefully catch a cab. The corridors had emptied quickly; it was getting late, and I figured most of the students were probably done for the day.

I made my way through the empty corridor for a while before realizing it curved around on itself and didn't appear to have an external door. Hearing music from the end of the hall, I decided to keep going in the hopes that someone could point me in the right direction. As I grew closer, I realized that it wasn't just any song that was playing, but one of Thorns's songs—the only one that I had written for our new album.

Before Chase had become involved, we only had a couple of usable tunes, one of which I had penned. The song was titled "Galaxies," and though it wasn't the most recognizable track on the sophomore record, it was meaningful to me, and our hard-core fans still knew the words by heart. When we played it in large theaters and stadiums, we encouraged the audience to shine the flashlights on their phones up at the stage. The vast auditoriums looked like they were filled with stars, and it was always a beautiful moment in the show.

I poked my nose into the room where the music was coming from, and my breath caught in my throat. A lone dancer flew through the air, graceful and perfectly in sync with the lyrics Carter sang. Reacting physically, I leaned in closer, completely in awe of the scene in front of me.

The dance studio itself was unassuming. A row of full-length mirrors covered one wall, with ballet barres lining the others, except for some space next to the door where there were shelves for students to store their things. A couple of posters above the shelves featured ballerinas in pointe shoes, with motivational sayings. The floor was black, and the ceiling was lofty, with speakers embedded high in the corners so you could hear the music from wherever you happened to be.

The dancer was breathtaking. He wore next to nothing—a simple pair of nude boy shorts that left very little to the imagination—but surprisingly his outfit wasn't what captured my attention. The lines of his body were so fluid as he progressed through the dance. His movements were impossibly complex. Yet he made them look effortless. He was wild but controlled. Purposeful though animalistic. Graceful and masculine. A jumble of contradictions that fought logic and gender norms in a beautiful display of dynamism. The power he radiated from every muscle and tendon was paralyzing.

The dancer's core was a perfect six-pack. His body was sculpted by practical use, not only for show, chiseled out of exercising for a living instead of hours spent ballooning at the gym. His legs extended each time he jumped; even his toes were stretching and pointing. His arms were long and elegant, holding tension and shifting around an invisible partner.

The piece was a duet. I could see that now from his movements. The passion he conveyed in every motion, every *breath*, was a fervent expression of desire. I had never been particularly enthusiastic about staged dance routines—they had always seemed dry and pompous to me, much like playing the piano instead of the keyboard—but the way this man showcased his body to a rock song shattered every preconception in my mind.

And it was *sexy*.

My God, the strength needed to lift and move himself so effortlessly captured my focus to the point that I didn't even notice when the music faded away and the song ended.

The dancer bent over and rested his hands on his knees. His chest rose and fell quickly as he fought to catch his breath from the vigorous feat. After a moment he stood and ran his fingers through his hair, drawing my attention to it. Despite his exertion the dancer's hair was still perfectly coiffed. It was the most beautiful color of mahogany red, longer on the top than the sides in a pompadour style. His locks were complemented by a well-maintained short beard that I had the immediate desire to feel scraping across my skin.

I shuddered involuntarily at the thought.

As he was already covered in a light sheen of sweat, it didn't take much to slot this man into the fantasy category. His intense blue eyes flickered up in the mirror, sensing my presence and, embarrassingly, noticing me drooling over him. Despite the feeling of being caught with my hand in the cookie jar, I couldn't force myself to look away. A crease furrowed his brow as he turned to face me, replaced a second later by a look of recognition.

"Holy shit, you're Beau Davis," he told me.

While I had grown somewhat accustomed to being recognized in public, it was never as frequent for me as it was for Carter, or when I was out with a second band member. It still threw me off a little when it happened. It was weird that people knew who I was. With overly enthusiastic fans, I had a hard time deciding exactly how I should react. In general, I mostly kept to myself, preferring to relax with a book or a movie after a concert instead of tracking down parties and groupies with my bandmate Dean.

"I am." I chuckled out loud at his assessment. "Sorry for barging in. I got lost and heard music down the hall. That was… wow… that was amazing," I said, struggling to adequately express how moved I was by what I had seen.

His blue eyes sparkled, and he grinned at me. He moved closer to the doorframe I had somehow become glued to.

"Thank you. It's still a work in progress. Obviously. But that's so cool you liked it. I'm Jamie, by the way." He extended his hand for a shake.

It was such a simple gesture—the smallest, most mundane amount of contact. Nonetheless, feeling his skin for the first time gave me butterflies. His hands were smooth and soft, unlike my own calloused musician's hands. I caught myself staring at our joined hands, feeling a little slow because of his touch.

"Oh, sorry," he said, looking down at the expanse of his bare chest, likely assuming that was what I was gaping at.

Now that he'd drawn my attention to it, I couldn't take my eyes off his torso. Jamie plucked a T-shirt off of the floor and pulled it over his head at leisure, seemingly unbothered by his own nakedness. I looked up to meet his gaze, pretending I hadn't been ogling him.

"So what are you doing here at Juilliard?" He asked.

I forced myself out of my stupor, trying to focus and be a coherent conversationalist.

"Oh, um, I was a guest at one of the first-year music classes. A favor to a friend of mine," I replied, still feeling sluggish and stupidly affected by this stranger in front of me.

"Cool. The students must have loved having you," he said, smile easy and warm.

"I dunno about that." I laughed. "I think I'm a little too rough around the edges for the Juilliard crowd."

"Some of us like it rough." He winked at me.

My face got hot from his blatant flirting; I had no idea how to respond. No way did he know how accurate that statement was. Right?

"But seriously," Jamie continued, smirking at my flustered reaction, "they need a shake-up when they first get here. They're always too classical. Too focused on the rules. Nothing great comes out of simply copying what someone else does."

The unexpected profoundness of Jamie's statement affected me. I had never been formally trained or had aspirations to be any type of prim and proper musician. Not that there was anything wrong with that; it just wasn't who I was or a part of the opportunities I had been given in life. Ever since I'd walked into the building earlier, I had felt *less than*. Less than trained. Less than classy. Less than part of the elite—which was ridiculous, because I made more money and had more fans than I knew what to do with. Yet I couldn't help but think back to a time when that hadn't been the case.

It had been a weird day all around.

"Hey, so I'm sure you've got stuff to do, and you probably get this all the time, but any chance I can buy you a drink and ask you a few questions about your music?" Jamie asked. "There's a couple bits of this piece I'm struggling with, and it would be amazing to get your opinion." He ran a towel over his face and began throwing his stuff into a bag.

Something about Jamie was calling out to me. Obviously he was gorgeous, but I was drawn to him for other reasons I couldn't fully describe. I had no idea why I was so fascinated by him. All I knew was there was no way I was going to pass up a chance to spend more time in the company of this captivating man.

"I'm not much of a dancer. Not sure I'd be any help." I smiled self-consciously. "But yeah, I've got some time."

Jamie

"**YOU** didn't!" Beau exclaimed, laughing uninhibitedly over the top of his second beer.

"Totally did. So after I came offstage, the costume designer and the director called me over and chewed my ass off about the changes I made to my outfit. They *did* stop short of firing me on the spot—probably because they didn't want to teach someone else the part overnight. But the review in the *Times* the next day specifically raved about how my outfit was the perfect dramatic paradox— that's what they said: "dramatic paradox"—for the piece. Long, *long* story short, that plus an injury made me decide that telling people what to do is way better than being told. Creating my own shit is more fun than dancing the stuffy old *Nutcracker* every year for eternity."

"So you became a choreographer," Beau concluded.

"So I became a choreographer." I nodded. "And now those pretentious pricks keep me employed because I do my job well and they're terrified of me leaving to go work for another company. Plus they take care of the boring admin crap like getting the licensing rights to use the music, so I can't complain too much."

I paused to take a sip of my drink. "Ballet isn't just classical pieces anymore. It can be modern. Lyrical. Emotional and exciting. Contemporary dance is every bit as important as the *Swan Lakes* of the world. It makes people feel and connect. Sometimes it's easier to express yourself and tell a story with movement instead of words."

Yes, I was aware I probably sounded cocky as fuck to the Grammy-winning, world-class musician sitting beside me on his bar stool, but I couldn't help it. Talking about dance—especially my type of dance—brought out the passion in me, and it was hard to remember to tone it down when I got on a roll.

"Wow, that's amazing. Now that you mention it, I vaguely remember going through the music rights for stuff like that with our agent. Guess I hadn't really thought about it. I had no idea people actually do, like, choreography to Thorns's songs. Dancing at a club or something, yeah. But what you did in there? That was something else." Beau's soulful brown eyes were wide.

Tonight was a trip. I had no idea how I'd ended the night in my local bar talking to this crazy-talented man. Inevitable Thorns was one of my all-time favorite bands. I had choreographed to a couple of their pieces over the years. Their music seemed to lend itself perfectly to the way I liked to create movement: fluid, with an intensity behind it. Melodic but filled with edge and angst. The

Thorns songs were filled with stories of love and tragedy, more akin to opera than a lot of the crap on the radio today.

The piece I had been working on earlier was one of the lesser-known songs on their latest album. That was another thing I loved—not sticking to the single or the obvious choice for the music. It was like bringing new life to a piece that might be forgotten over time. "Galaxies" was just as deserving of accolades as any of Thorns's bigger hits, but there were simply too many good tracks in their catalog for all of them to become sensations.

"I'm really happy you liked it. Like I said, it's still a work in progress."

I raised my glass to my lips to take a gulp of the cool liquid.

"Can I ask you something?" I asked, not wanting to squander the opportunity to talk to Beau about his music. He nodded and gestured for me to go on. "So I guess I'm just trying to figure out how to play the ending. It's so ambiguous in the final verse. I know that he leaves his lover because of the hurt she's caused, but there's still hope there too. Does that mean she eventually gets better? Do they find their way back to each other?"

He smiled at me, seemingly enjoying listening to my interpretation of the lyrics his band had written.

"What?" I finally asked. I furrowed my brow, self-consciousness getting the best of me. "I'm not that far off, am I?"

"No, not far off." Beau stroked his chin before continuing slowly. "I guess I don't really know about the ending. I did need to leave to get out of a bad situation, but I'm always optimistic that the other person will eventually find their way. Not so we can be together. For themself. So it *is* kind of ambiguous, in my mind at least. The listener can interpret it as either cautiously hopeful for the future or the end of the relationship."

I thought for a moment about that unhelpful comment. Vagueness wasn't the worst thing in the world, but I wished Beau had a clearer answer. There was something about the piece that called out to me. I got the sense that I was circling the spark, the magic. It seemed to be just outside my grasp, but I couldn't put my finger on what exactly *it* was.

"But, um… it's not about a she," Beau added quietly. "At least it wasn't when I wrote it."

I paused for a second, genuinely caught off guard.

"Oh shit, seriously?" I asked. "You're gay?"

"Bi, actually. But this song was about a guy. I didn't, like, purposely leave out pronouns or anything, they just didn't work into the lyrics. I kinda liked how it turned out, not weighed down by answers or concrete details. Or gender. It's not a song that gets talked about much, so nobody's really asked us during interviews or anything."

Egoistically I was far more engrossed by the new ideas this admission generated for my choreography than about Beau's personal confession. Even before I consciously thought it through, I knew immediately that this was the flame I had been looking for. My head was spinning.

The piece I had been creating was a typical duet between a man and a woman. I had already mentally cast the male lead, but I was having a hard time deciding who the female should be. This revelation offered the opportunity to change things.

I suddenly felt alive with possibility. My blood pumped rapidly through my body, thumping loudly in my ears. The skin on my arms grew tight with goose bumps, and my whole body vibrated with the creative energy that was flowing. Now that the idea was embedded, I couldn't picture the number as a traditional male/female pas de deux anymore.

It needed to be danced by two men.

Fuck.

It *needed* to be danced by two men.

www.dreamspinnerpress.com

FOR
MORE
OF THE
BEST
GAY
ROMANCE

DREAMSPINNER
PRESS
dreamspinnerpress.com

www.ingramcontent.com/pod-product-compliance
Lightning Source LLC
Chambersburg PA
CBHW030312200626
46816CB00002BA/873